To Whi

Best Wishes.

Diana

Dec. 2022.

1

To my late husband Peter: thank you for your support in this project, as in all things. The long walks populated with characters, plot twists and red herrings fill my head, my heart, and this book with wonderful memories.

Death By Degree

An Inspector Daffyd Jones Novel

By
Diana Anstead

PROLOGUE

I noticed the car as I turned the corner and drove down the quiet road towards the church. He had parked on the road, within the shadow of the large oak tree. He stared as I turned into the parking lot but then quickly drove in and drew up beside me sending grit rattling against my side window. I resisted his gestures for me to get in his car instead I leant across, opened my passenger door and waved him in. I prayed that my nervousness was not apparent as I knew that if my plan was to work, if I was to dictate the course of events then I had to remain totally unemotional. Finally, he opened his door, climbed out and stood waiting. Obviously, he was not happy at the prospect of getting into my car. I waited determined not to give way. Reluctantly he climbed into my passenger seat and slammed the door. His cold, icy blue eyes stared at me.

"Well?" He asked.

"I have hurt my knee and it's difficult for me to climb in and out," I explained.

"Hmm, well where is it?"

"First I have some information that you should see," I said as I started to lean over to retrieve the envelope from the back seat but as I stretched and put my left arm over the back of his seat to reach out I swung my right arm across my body and drove the needle hard into his thigh. With my body stretched out against him he hadn't seen the syringe coming. Within seconds he sat motionless, only his eyes showing the fear and panic that I knew he felt as the paralytic drug started to take effect. I leant across him and locked his door. I certainly didn't want him falling out. Staying calm, I put the car into Drive, pulled away from the church turning cautiously onto the main road. I didn't look at my passenger, I had no need, I knew what the drug would do, and it served him right

Striving to keep my nerves under control, I drove carefully down the road until turning into a dark laneway. Stopping at the back of the summerhouse which I knew was hidden from view by the large evergreen trees. Dragging him out of the car and into the carefully placed wheelbarrow was almost too much for me. I struggled for breath as I wheeled the heavy load into the summerhouse, through the hidden door and down into the *tunnel. He would be safe down there I thought as I turned my back on the sightless eyes. Once out in the fresh air I drove my car to a quiet parking spot near the village bus stop, walked back to the church and with his keys drove his car back to his parking place in Church Road. Leaving his keys on the floor of his car, I slipped out the side entrance just in time to catch the bus to Steyning where I picked up my car and drove home. I had completed the first phase of my plan and in two days I would return to Baxter House and give my tormentor the finality he deserved...*

CHAPTER ONE

Caught by the wind, the umbrella turned inside out leaving its owner feeling the full force of the sleet on her face.

"Oh damn," Phyllis said turning her back to the wind hoping to turn the umbrella the right way. But a gust sent it out of her hand, across the road into the gutter where it was hastily swept up by the rushing water and sent spinning down the hill to join the rest of the flotsam steadily floating towards the large drain in the middle of the road.

"Oh it's going to be one of those days?" she thought as she turned up her coat collar and retied her headscarf under her chin in an attempt to keep her hair dry at least until she'd covered the final few steps to the office door.

"Come in, come in Phyllis," said her boss, "Let's have a warm cup of tea before we start for the day."

Thankfully Phyllis took off her sodden coat, carried it through to the tiny area that served as a bathroom and hung the dripping garment over the door trailing the lower half into the sink to catch the drips. A quick glance in the small mirror confirmed that the rain had caused her hair to tie itself up into tiny curls and she could do nothing about it until it dried out. In the even smaller kitchen Mr. Trent had placed three mugs and the tea caddy ready for the boiling water.

"I don't expect we'll get many interested people in today Phyllis," he said

"No, Mr. Trent, who wants to look at houses in weather like this?" Phyllis took two tea-filled mugs into the office. The third agent hadn't arrived yet but then Stella had much further to walk. "Perhaps Stella will make it before the tea is stewed. Oooh this is so good," she said wrapping her hands around the warm mug. Just then the telephone on her desk rang.

"Trent Estate Agents, can I help you?" answered Phyllis.

"Today?" she grimaced at Mr. Trent, "What time could you be here? Fine we will see you at noon today. What name is it? Thank you." Phyllis finished her note and turned to Mr. Trent.

"A Mr. Walker wants to see the Baxter house over in Ditchling. He will be here at noon today."

"Oh dear," said Trent, "I have to go out this afternoon, so you'll have to take him up there. Take the car and be sure to put on your Wellingtons as it will be very muddy up there today." Trent went across to pick up some papers.

"Phyllis when was the last time anybody wanted to view Baxter House?"

"It has to be at least three months. I am surprised anybody would want such a broken-down place. I wonder if it's a developer who is more interested in the six acres of land, than the house."

"Possibly, but why now? Why not two years ago when it first came on the market? Will you be alright then on your own?"

"Yes. I will be fine, and Stella will be here in the office if I need help. But he'd better be serious about buying, dragging me out there in this kind of weather."

Trent's Estate Agency was located in a row of shops along the main road; in fact, it was the only road that ran through the village of Steyning in Sussex. The Agency's clientele were mostly people who wanted to get out of the hurly burly of nearby Brighton or away from London and all its post-war difficulties. Steyning offered good rail connections to the main service to Brighton and then to London; the village also offered the opportunity to live in a community that prided itself on its quiet respectability and reputable trade opportunities. Maurice Trent now owned Trent Estate Agency, as had his late father before him. Trent employed two qualified agents, Phyllis and Stella, and a secretary who came in three days a week to do the filing and the books. Trent was not one for the fast paced life of city agents, what he wanted was a steady, successful business that provided him with enough income to look after his wife and three boys, and allow him to indulge in his passion of watching or playing cricket.

The prospective buyer walked into the office at precisely two minutes to twelve.

"Mr. Walker?' asked Phyllis.

"Yes." Walker was middle-aged, perhaps in his fifties; he was tall, sturdily built, with a mass of gray hair that was surprisingly long for a man his age. Dressed in a yellow sou'wester and Wellington boots he was well prepared for the afternoon's trek out to Baxter House. Phyllis picked up a Trent Agency folder, pulled on her still-damp coat, wriggled into her Wellington boots and said,

"Shall we go then?"

"I have my car at the curb so we could use that if you liked?" suggested Walker.

Phyllis hesitated; although she had never had an adverse experience, she was still wary of being on her own with a male buyer, in an empty lonely house, without any means of escape. But she also prided herself on her judgment of people and she thought that Walker seemed safe, so she agreed. It would save a long, wet walk around to where Mr. Trent had parked the office car. Once they were on their way out of Steyning Phyllis opened her folder and began her spiel.

"This house has been on the market for two years. The owner, an elderly man died and left it to his niece but as she had already moved to Canada, it was rented on her behalf. When the last tenant died the niece wanted the property sold. It is large, with five bedrooms and two bathrooms on the top floor, three spacious living rooms on the ground floor with a recessed kitchen at the back. Is this the type of property you want Mr. Walker?"

"Tell me about the land," asked Walker.

"Ah we thought that might be where your interest lay. There is approximately ten acres of meadow with a small orchard at the south end."

"Has it ever been fully worked?"

"Only as a small holding. The man had lived there all his life as had his father. Here, we are turn right at that post; the house sits up on a knoll at the end of the path. Through there," she directed, pointing towards the mass of cedar trees that faced them.

The Baxter House looked like something out of an architect's nightmare. The east wing was the original early eighteenth century Georgian building, still wearing the evidence of the fire that destroyed the rest of the house, while the west wing had been rebuilt in a particularly ugly Victorian style. The woodwork was originally painted gray, but time and weather had joined forces to remove most of the paint leaving just the hint of black on the wood. But the leaded windows were all intact the main entrance was a double wooden cathedral-shaped door with ring handles. Phyllis struggled to open the door. The enormous black iron key fitted well but it took a strong wrist to get it turned and then to push the door open. The inside was as decaying as the outside, most of the doors were ajar and the rooms appeared to be full of large pieces of furniture covered in dustsheets. Cobwebs swayed as the draught from the front door caught their delicate strands. There were mice droppings on the floor; an upstairs door banged continuously and there was a horrible fetid smell. Phyllis drew a sharp breath.

"Oh dear, this place smells funny, it isn't just stale, there's something else. Oh dear, perhaps an animal got in and died. Let's leave the big door open and I'll open a couple of windows." Mr. Walker stood looking around sniffing the air.

"Hmm, funny smell that. We'll have to track that down. Must be the drains or something like that. Now I see that some of the furniture is still here," he said running his hand across the highly polished oak hall table.

"Yes. Everything is included in the price of the house or if it's not wanted, we can send it to auction and make arrangements about a refund. It really is too good to just throw away. We will do whatever the client wants," finished Phyllis. She opened her folder, "Shall we start down here with the reception rooms?" she suggested. Together agent and client worked their way through the four large reception rooms. Each room had been furnished and decorated with a particular function in mind. The first room at the front of the house looked out across a large lawn bordered by the traditional herbaceous plants although sadly neglected, shades of its past splendour were still apparent. This room held a large double pedestal oak desk which was placed under the front window ideally situated to see who was coming to visit. The second room was facing the back and was decorated with a great deal of green chintzy covered, less formal furniture. The view was spectacular across the sloping garden and then the meadow leading down to the brook.

They must have wanted to bring the garden into the house," commented Walker, "certainly a comfortable sitting room."

The next room, also facing the back was a reading room with two of its walls covered by bookshelves, although the books themselves were few and far between. The last reception room was totally empty of furniture although velvet curtains still hung at the windows. The kitchen was very large, and Phyllis pointed out that the kitchen window gave an excellent view of the property. Off to the left was a glass summerhouse and then further down the slope stood a large shed. Phyllis checked her folder realizing that there was still another room on this floor.

"I did forget to show you the small room off the second reception room and that was used as an office. Shall we go and look?" Walker was ahead of Phyllis; he turned the door handle, stepped in and came to a sudden stop. Phyllis who was behind had her head down looking at her notes and bumped heavily into his back.

"What's the matter?" she asked, trying to get round him. Walker put out his arm and blocked her from moving.

"Just a minute now, what are you up to?" she asked pushing him away. "Oh, what is that smell? It's making me sick," she asked over his shoulder. Walker turned, grabbed her shoulders and physically turned her around and pushed her out of the doorway.

"You do not want to go in there believe me. I'm sorry I pushed you, but it was necessary. Come over here and sit down and I will tell you what I saw. But first is there a telephone nearby?"

"Yes, we left the one in the kitchen connected up."

"I will telephone the police. Please do not go into the room or you'll have nightmares for years to come. Better still," he took her arm, "walk with me to the telephone." Phyllis could see by Walker's pale face that he had been shocked by what he had seen in the room and noticed the shaken man needed both hands to hold the instrument steady.

"Operator? Get me the police at once."

"Steyning sub-police station Sgt. Hewitt speaking." Walker explained where he was and why he and Phyllis were there. Then he demanded that an officer be sent out immediately to take charge of what he knew to be a case of murder. Walker and Phyllis sat on the staircase and waited for the police to arrive.

"You know I have seen dead bodies before. I was a volunteer ambulance driver for St. John's and sometimes I moved bodies into the vehicles," said Phyllis.

"I will tell you what I saw if you really want to know?" Phyllis nodded. "As you said the room was an office and there is a large desk over by the window." Phyllis nodded again. Walker took a deep breath "And on that desk was a pair of human arms holding a book, as a person would do when reading."

"So?" asked Phyllis.

"There was no body, just the arms and hands around the book," finished Walker.

Phyllis stared at him then abruptly bent over and tried desperately to hold on to her morning tea. Pulling out her handkerchief and holding it to her mouth she sat there rocking, just staring at Walker. They heard the siren at the same moment, and both sets of shoulders relaxed knowing that somebody else would now take over and they could leave. Phyllis remained seated on the lower staircase as Walker moved across to the open front door to greet the policeman.

"Morning Sir. I am Sgt. Hewitt. Who are you and what is the problem?" asked the big, burly uniformed man as he stepped through the door. Walker explained who he was and why he was there. The Sgt. acknowledged Phyllis, who was still sat on the stairs.

"Afternoon Miss Wilcott, is what the gentleman says true?" Phyllis nodded; she couldn't trust herself to speak yet. Walker then pointed to the office door and strongly suggested that the Sgt. take a look in there.

"I have seen enough I do not want to go in there again," said Walker.

"Why do you think it's murder, sir, and not just an accident?" asked Hewitt.

"Just take one look and you will not ask that question again."

The Sgt. turned on his heel, called sharply to the young constable who came in with him and purposefully strode across to the office door all the while muttering about 'busybodies'. Moments later they both emerged, an ashen-faced Sgt. supporting the young constable, while attempting to hold a handkerchief to his own face. He gestured to Walker

"Please take young Owens outside. I will make sure that C.I.D. is on the way."

It was a long half an hour before more sirens were heard, cars were parked, and heavy footsteps came up what passed for the front path and three men in raincoats came through the still open door. Sgt. Hewitt got up from his place on the stairs and introduced himself and Constable Owens to the newcomers. Without delay Sgt. Hewitt led them to the office door and then waited outside. Seconds later three-stone faced men came out and moved slowly across to where Phyllis and her client waited. It was the taller man who spoke first.

"Thank you for waiting for us. I am Detective Inspector Daffyd Jones, this is Det. Sgt Smith, and this is Det. Constable Masters. Please sit down and tell us what happened."

"I am Phyllis Wilcott and I work for Trent Estate Agency on the High Street. We have this house on our books and Mr. Walker wanted to see it this morning. We looked in the four reception rooms and the kitchen and we were going into that one, the small office Mr. Walker happened to be in front and as he opened the door he suddenly put his arm out to stop me going in, and that's about all."

"And you Sir?"

"I am Mr. Robert Walker. I work for Brown's Building Company and we are interested in buying this property for future development. Miss Wilcott has told you exactly how things happened this afternoon. Oh, I did tell Miss Wilcott what was in that room?" Inspector Jones nodded his thanks and explained.

"My officers and I are just going to do a search of the entire house to see if there are any more surprises. Do you mind waiting? Outside in my car if you wish." But both Phyllis and Walker preferred to wait on the stairs. Each of the four officers moved out into different parts of the house to search while Constable Owens telephoned for an ambulance. Before long they were back downstairs conferring, then Inspector Jones strode across to the waiting couple.

"We are going to be here for a while yet. If you have given your names and addresses to Constable Masters, you are free to leave although we might be in touch later for a statement."

"Were there anymore?" asked Walker.

"Yes, I'm afraid so, we found enough parts to make a complete body." With that he thanked them for their patience and said goodbye.

Jones pulled away the dustsheets covering a large dining table and chairs to use as a temporary command post. Sgt Smith had called back to Brighton for a photographer, a forensic team and extra uniformed officers while confirming that a medical examiner was on the way. But now Jones noticed that his sergeant appeared to be in some distress. The older man was as white as a ghost and sat leaning on his elbows with his head between his hands. Jones walked around to him.

"What is it Jack? What's wrong?"

"I know who the victim is sir, I wasn't sure at first but now I know for sure."

"Is it a friend?"

"No, never a friend but a former colleague. The victim is ex-Police Sergeant Ray Blount, late of the Sussex Constabulary."

"Good God. Retired?"

"No." Smith shook his head, "Booted out." Jones was silent, he knew any other questions about the victim could wait but now he had to go out to the car to let his superintendent know who the victim was.

CHAPTER TWO

Smith stood up as soon as Jones came back." I'm all right now Sir, it was a shock when I recognized who it was." Smith pushed his chair back under the table and stood up, "What now?" Jones saw that the photographer had arrived, He asked Smith to go with the photographer and make sure that every part of the victim's body was photographed as it was found, as well as the rooms themselves.

"Are you okay with that Jack?" he asked.

But Smith was already striding across the room to take charge of the photographer. As Jones walked in and out of the rooms on the main floor he was checking his notes: the arms and hands, holding a book in the office, the legs with feet still attached, upside down in the bed with just the feet visible on the pillow, the torso with the head still attached propped up in a Queen Anne chair in another bedroom.

"At least it was partially covered by a blanket!" thought Jones. Remnants of clothing still clung to the individual body parts, but Jones had to wait for the Medical Examiner before anything could be moved. The ME could give an approximation on how long the victim had been dead.

"Damn good job that lady and her client didn't go upstairs," he muttered to himself.

Inspector Dai Jones was thirty years old, young to hold the rank of Inspector but long experienced in the matter of policing, both as a probationary constable in York and then as a detective with the Liverpool Force. Taller than the average policeman at six foot two inches, his broad shoulders carried his slim frame with a stance reminiscence of his military training. He had a long face which naturally carried a stern look, but when he smiled, which was often, his brown eyes lit up, his firm white teeth sparkled transforming his face into one that inspired confidence. Jones wore his hair longer than the traditional 'short back and sides' with one stubborn wave that always fell down over his forehead to cover a three-inch white scar that ran across his left eyebrow. A memento of a childhood scrumping adventure, of which he seemed inordinately proud.

Jones' family roots were in South Wales but after a mining accident that killed both his father and grandfather, Jones was determined to leave the valley and everything about mining behind. His move to the Sussex coast was the result of an unexpected offer of promotion. In Liverpool his colleague and best friend had been shot while pursuing a burglar and when he asked his girlfriend to go to Sussex with him, she refused to even consider moving.

By the time the photographer and Smith returned to the dining room Jones had assigned four uniformed officers to search the entire house and grounds. He knew that it would take a couple of days to get every room searched and its contents listed in detail, but in the time remaining before dark he needed to be sure that there were no other human remains anywhere on the property.

Masters was detailed to go around the outside of the house and check for unexplained tire tracks. Jones really didn't hold out much hope for any success as it had rained four out of the past five days. Jones had been reluctant to send young Masters out in the pouring rain as he had only recently returned to full duties after suffering a gunshot wound to the chest. But Masters was extremely knowledgeable about cars and being keen to get back into action he'd jumped at the chance to be of help. Smith had completed his work with the photographer who joined Masters outside taking photos of the small outbuildings and any tracks that Masters found.

Jones, Smith and Dr. Marshall, the Medical Examiner, sat at the round table

"I was wondering if either of you noticed the title of the book that lay between the hands on the desk?" asked Smith.

"No, I didn't turn it over. Why what was it?"

"It was Crime and Punishment by that Russian fellow. That could mean something about the motive."

"Hmmp. Interesting," said the other men.

"Now then what do we have doc.?" asked Jones

"From my preliminary examination the body pieces belong to the same man. I would judge that the body had been here about a month but as there are no bloodstains in the vicinity of any of the individual parts I would say that the dismembering was done after death had occurred."

"Was it done here?" asked Jones.

"Very difficult to say." The doctor shuffled in his seat. "To be certain we would need to find signs of a large amount of blood in a place where a man's body could be laid out flat. The cutting certainly did not take place on the bed, no signs of anything I checked right through to the frame and the floor beneath."

"Any opinion on how it was done?"

"Once again, preliminary examination would lead me to suspect the tool was an axe as the cuts are blunt. I can tell you more once I have the body in my lab." Dr. Marshall rose, "Is it ready for release?"

"Yes," said Jones, "but we'll be over tomorrow afternoon to see what else you can tell us."

Jones and Smith watched as the ambulance men went from room to room gathering up the grisly remains of ex- Sgt. Ray Blount. By the time they left, the attendants, both young men, were looking decidedly pale. Sgt. Hewitt had escorted the men and now returned to Jones for further instructions.

"How many men do you have out here Sgt?"

"Five sir; myself and four constables."

"Good I need someone out here to secure this building at least until tomorrow night. Do you have someone?"

"Yes. I will send out Constable Pierce, he is a little older and entirely reliable. He can have a car out here and then he can report in every couple of hours. Are you expecting anything to happen then sir?"

Jones shrugged "I don't really know what to expect. It is a very bizarre case and perhaps the killer, having seen our cars here today will return to see what we have discovered. Who knows?"

"I will have Pierce here by six o'clock, will that be okay? Did you know the victim sir?"

"No, I didn't. But my sergeant did, and I expect some of the senior men at the station will have known him."

"A difficult time for all. We will help all we can at this end."

"Thank you. Much appreciated. Now we have more to do here and then we'll be leaving for the office, but we'll be back early tomorrow," said Jones.

Back in the drawing room Sgt. Smith, the historian noted. "This must have been a grand house in its time, with its solidly built, beautiful wood carvings around the ceilings and down the staircase. I imagine about eighty years ago it was the centre of society around here," he said. "Why would anyone just go away and leave all this expensive furniture and these paintings to deteriorate. You know sir," he said turning to Jones, "it's surprising that tramps or kids haven't been in here messing around, but not a sign of anything living, just a dead one, in pieces. Sorry."

By five o'clock, Masters had reported that his search had, indeed, been fruitless, nothing resembling human anatomical parts had been discovered in any of the outer buildings and the photographer had left. Jones, Smith and Sgt. Hewitt, made plans for a more thorough search the following day. Sgt. Hewitt suggested that if the Inspector wanted to leave, he would wait the hour for Constable Pierce to arrive.

"Excellent we will go into the village and see if we can catch the Estate agent before she leaves her office, perhaps she can tell us more about the owners of this house." Before Smith could respond Jones had his raincoat and boots on and was through the front door heading to their car. Smith called out.

"What about Masters, he came out with us?"

"Oh right. Tell him to get a lift from one of the uniforms. I'll wait in the car for you."

It was almost closing time when the officers walked into Trent's Agency. Phyllis recognized them immediately and introduced both Jones and Smith to Mr. Trent.

"What a rum deal out there this afternoon, Miss Wilcott told me all about it. Have you finished out there now?" asked Trent.

"No, we will be at least another day finishing up the details. But we stopped by as we need some history on this property and thought perhaps you could help us out, and we needed to see that Miss Wilcott had recovered from her fright." Jones said turning to Phyllis.

"Oh, I'm okay thanks; at least I didn't see it so it's only my own imagination I have to worry about."

"That's good," he said and took a seat by Trent's desk.

"Let me see," said Trent opening a manila file. "Ah, now I remember. We received instruction from Mr. Siddely, a solicitor in Hove, to sell the house on behalf of the beneficiary of the former owner's will, a Mrs. James, who now lives in Canada and has no need for the house. We've had Baxter House on our books for two years although I believe it was empty for a while before that. We have shown it to prospective buyers but just four times with the last showing back in the spring and of course today's client."

"Apart from yourself who else would have a key to the house?"

"To my knowledge we are the only ones. Phyllis show the Inspector the key."

Phyllis opened her draw and pulled out a large black iron key.

"Really it's more like a church door key than a house key," she commented. Jones agreed and passing it to Smith suggested that not many people would carry a key this weight around with them.

"Was it a break-in?" asked Trent.

"There were no visible signs of forcible entrance in any of the buildings or damage to the furnishings," Jones replied. "But what we need now is the address and telephone number of Mr. Siddely if you would?" Phyllis passed over a small card with the details and Jones and Smith left.

"Well?" asked Jones as they walked back to the car...

"Seems like an ordinary country Estate Agents. They were all eager to help. But did you get a look at the price of some of the homes up for sale, pretty expensive to live out here."

"Yes. I was just thinking that when we start questioning the locals, I wonder how helpful they will be. In a village like this they would never think that the killer could be one of them."

"You're right there. Everyone will believe that the killer was an outsider who just made use of the house to display his work?"

"Well one thing we all know is that whoever did the killing was in an absolute rage about something the victim did, or they believed he did."

CHAPTER THREE

Supt. Young was already waiting at the door when Jones got back to his office.

"Tell me all you know. I never liked the man, he was a bully and a liar, and I was part of the panel that fired him, but nobody deserves this indignity."

Young shook his head as he sat; he was visibly shaken by the afternoon's events. Jones relayed everything that had happened in Steyning, giving details about where and how each body part was displayed. He also explained about the remaining work that would be done at the site next morning and gave some background of the Baxter house.

"Any leads yet?" asked the still shaken Super.

"Nothing obvious. My first job is to find out whether he was known locally. The doc. couldn't find any sign in the house that the killing or dismemberment took place there, so we must go further afield. And that means that particular house was either just convenient or there was some specific connection to the killer and the crime. Of course, we now have to search here, at the station for his old files, and see what we can turn up about his activities. But I know that what he did, or was thought to have done, must have been pretty horrific to end up like he has."

"What a day this is turning out to be," complained Young. "It is enough that our new A.C.C. has been prowling around today and now this."

"God he's hardly been here five minutes and he has everybody on edge. What's he all in a twist about now?" asked Jones.

"It seems he feels that our reporting system is not up to scratch so he is going to invent a new more efficient method. He hasn't spoken to me about it, but he and the C.C. are often in conversation. You know that he is actually a distant relation to our Chief Constable?"

"Yes, I had heard that piece of good news! Anyway, thanks for the heads up." Young was still ranting when Smith walked in to see Jones "As if having an ambitious, dogmatic ACC wasn't bad enough now we have the horrific murder of a sacked detective on our hands.

He'll love this one and it will give him more ammunition to think that this station is inefficient. It's a good job that he is uniform and cannot interfere with our investigation. Although I'm sure he'll do his best to have some say in how we do business."

Sgt. Jack Smith was a family man who had spent his entire policing career at the same station. He had never particularly sought promotion but just as the war became a reality he was approached by his Supt. and asked to take a position in the CID. It was more interesting than he first thought and by the time Jones came along Smith had the department working as efficiently as possible given the post-war shortages of just about everything including staff.

At first, he had been very leery about Jones' ability to hold the position of inspector at such a young age. But during the weeks on their first case together Smith had come to accept Jones as being an intelligent, empathetic, hardworking policeman. Together they had made even more improvements to the communication system, especially the daily reports, and this had built up a good trust factor between head office and the smaller substations.

"Let's hope he keeps out of our way," answered Smith.

Blount's last known address turned out to be in a small terraced house on short road just above the local Intermediate School. Apparently, Blount had the upstairs floor while the owner lived in the ground floor flat, but Blount had moved out a few years ago, much to Mrs. Humphries' delight. The landlady was a friendly woman and willingly admitted to Smith that she'd never liked Blount.

"I never felt comfortable around him," she said, "I was afraid of him and avoided meeting with him. I made my hubby collect his rent. I was not at all sorry when he left." She handed Smith the address that Blount had left saying,

"Don't know how he manages a flat in Church Road. Must have come into some money"

"Do you know if he had any family?" asked Smith.

"The only thing he ever mentioned to my husband was that he was married once, that's all," she said.

Smith and Jones drove out of Brighton into the adjacent town of Hove. A community whose citizens considered themselves much more sophisticated and cultured than the working-class folk of Brighton. Brighton was a great place to carry on a business whether commercial or trade, but the owners would never consider living in Brighton. A place full of railway workers or factory people. A town that at weekends became overwhelmed by families of day trippers, especially those from the East End of London, who found the hour-long railway journey from London both a cheap and convenient way of escaping the dirty air of the nation's capital. No, a Brighton address simply wasn't fashionable as a residence.

It didn't take the officers long to find Blount's latest address in Church Road. It was a block of luxury flats set back from the main road surrounded by well-maintained grounds.

"What on earth was Blount into that he could afford a place like this?" exclaimed Smith.

Entering through the glass doors they were met by a smartly dressed receptionist who enquired as to whom they were visiting. Jones and Smith looked at each other then showing their warrant cards and introducing themselves, asked to be shown flat number 6a. Despite the officer's authority the polite receptionist still insisted that they tell her the name of the tenant they were visiting. Jones reluctantly showed her a photo of Blount, in uniform.

"Oh yes that is our tenant, but he is not a policeman and his name is Mr. Ford. We believe he is abroad. Can you come back when he returns?"

"No," said Jones, "Now open that security door and allow us in. You may call your manager if you wish." She pressed a button under her desk and then quickly picked up her telephone, but the men were already through the door. As they went to enter the lift a short, stout man came running along the corridor.

"Wait, wait" he called out. "I am Mr. Hollingsworth the manager of these flats and I will let you into the flat, but I must accompany you to see that nothing is damaged. We have to be careful as our tenants pay a high rent to maintain their privacy."

The two officers just looked at each other neither trusting themselves to respond to this pompous little man. Once inside the flat the manager continued in his officious tone.

"I will stay here in case Mr. Ford returns, although he did leave without telling us." Jones turned to the short man and looking down at him patiently explained the situation.

"We have every reason to believe that your Mr. Ford will never, ever return to this flat."

"Oh, but he hasn't notified me of his leaving, and he is late with this month's rent. Anyway, how do you know he will not be coming back? Have you spoken to him?"

"No, we haven't spoken to Mr. Blount but believe me we know he will not be living here anymore." The man pouted but Jones had moved on.

"How did he pay his rent?"

"Oh dear." The little man protested," This is all very unusual. I don't know that I should be giving you this information without Mr. Ford's approval. This is so awkward."

"There is nothing awkward about this, just answer the question."

"Quarterly. Always in cash. He's been here about four years and never any problems," answered the still puzzled manager.

"Is this Mr. Ford's own furniture?"

"No, Mr. Ford had one of the few furnished flats that we rent. Some of the personal bits are his but the main furniture is ours." Turning his back to the manager Jones asked Smith,

"What do you think Sgt.?" Smith looked around the flat.

"I would like to know how a man with no pension or really any steady income at all, could afford this. I mean look at the quality of the furniture, the rent must be sky-high."

"I agree and I haven't seen anything that suggests he was running a business from here, have you?" asked Jones.

"Oh, Inspector we would never allow a tenant to do that here," was the indignant interruption from the manger.

"I suppose you needed references when he applied for a flat?" Jones asked.

"Absolutely. I can assure you that one doesn't get to live here unless one has impeccable references. If I remember correctly Mr. Ford gave a Sussex Police Superintendent as his reference and his occupation as being retired."

"Do you have the Superintendent's name?"

"Yes, I believe it was McLeod. I remember the name as I am Scottish too." Jones turned to Smith.

"Unfortunately, Supt. McLeod died three years ago," answered Smith, "no help there."

Jones decided that he had seen enough but told the manager that in all probability they would return for a second visit. The manager bristled.

"Not very good for our reputation to have the police in and out of our flats."

Smith responded with a sharp   "Let's hope, for your sake, that your Mr. Ford wasn't conducting anything illegal in this flat."

Mr. Hollingsworth looked horrified at this implication about one of his tenants and there was a tense silence as all three descended in the lift. The manager was so taken aback by their visit that he neglected to acknowledge the officers when they left his premise

"There is something very important about Blount that we are missing," Jones said as they walked towards their car. "I 'm sure that eventually we'll have to assign an officer to go through every case that he dealt with, to see if anything jumps out as being unusual about his investigations. Tomorrow we see Dr. Marshall at the morgue and then we'll have to see what money or bank accounts Blount had. I want you to ask around to see if any officers have any idea how he was making money these days. What is Masters doing tomorrow?"

"I am sending him back out to the house at Steyning to finish up."

"Good. He seems to be holding up well."

"Yes, he is so pleased to be back on full duties now. Lost some of his swagger though, perhaps tackling an armed man does alter one's outlook,"

Smith smiled as he remembered the young constable all trussed up in the hospital bed.

Next morning, when Jones was ready to go to the morgue, he was unable to find Sgt. Smith. Checking at the front desk he learnt that Smith was down in the basement with W.P.C. Jenkins, checking the archives for the cases that Blount had handled. Smith came hurriedly down the corridor.

"Sorry sir, I was helping Jenkins to get started on Blount's files. As you said sooner or later, we will need these details."

"Have you ever handled anything like this case in your time?" asked Jones as they walked together around the lawns of the Old Steine.

"There were some terrible cases during the bombing when people were literally blown apart and there were some who had limbs torn off and survived, but I have never seen anything as deliberate as this killing. Never," answered Smith.

Crossing at the lights Jones observed, "I think we're too tight for time to stop for coffee this morning, but I see the old man is there at his seat by the window. Do you know him Jack? Look he's tipping his cap at me even through the window, he does that every time I go in, and he's always there." Smith stepped closer to the window of Joe Lyons restaurant to get a good look at the man.

"Oh, I know him sir. He was done for horse doping up at the racecourse, a few years back now. He must have served his time and come back here to live. Harmless really, was taken advantage of by some London bookies, but he would never tell. I imagine he knows who you are and wants to let you know he's going straight now." said Smith.

Dr Marshall was waiting for them in his office adjacent to the hospital mortuary. He was dressed in a suit rather than his usual green surgical gown. He stepped out to greet them.

"Morning, we don't need to go into the laboratory today, come into my office. The photographer took some useful photos of our victim which helped me find the cause of death."

"Good," said a relieved Jones sitting in the chair closest to the desk, "I really appreciate not having to look at those actual body parts again. So, fire ahead. Tell us what you have discovered."

Dr. Marshall took a number of large black and white photographs out of his top draw and spread them across his desk facing the officers.

"The first three show exactly where each body part was found and the surrounding environment. The second group show the wounds left by the instrument used to dismember the body. But these final three are of special interest as they show the manner of death. They are of the torso and were taken here in the lab by my assistant yesterday afternoon."

"So, you were able to determine cause?" asked Jones.

"Yes indeed. Look closely at this first photo, no signs of injuries, no stab wounds or bruises, no bullet holes, no signs of strangulation or suffocation. And remember the dismembering was done after death." The doctor waited as the officers scrutinized the photos.

"I see that you are as surprised as I was. But it was under my microscope that I learnt the truth. Look closely at this second photo, just at the top of the thigh near the groin, do you see anything?"

"No" answered both officers.

"Then look at this close-up." He passed over another photo. "What do you see now?"

"A small hole, like an injection."

"Right. Your victim was killed by the injection of a drug which most probably put him in a coma and eventually killed him by some form of paralysis."

"Any sign of poison in his organs?"

"Yes, in both his stomach and his intestines I found minute traces of a substance common to all weed killer preparations. But as the blood had been allowed to drain away there was no outward sign of toxic poisoning. Had he been left whole I daresay he would have been quietly buried and nobody would be any wiser," said Dr. Marshall.

"Given the strength it would take to cut off the limbs of a man this size, are we looking for a man only?" asked Smith.

"Oh no," said the pathologist, "a woman could easily have wielded the axe, especially one driven by so much anger and revenge, adrenalin alone would have given her more strength. My own observation, if I may, would be that the motive is your real key to this case. Almost every household still maintains their wartime garden so weed killer can be found in hundreds of garden sheds, and a hypodermic needle can be bought over the counter at any chemist shop."

"So, we are looking for someone with knowledge of poisons, who knew of the house in Steyning and who had been badly treated by Blount. But a person who also knew that eventually Blount's remains would be found."

"I would suggest," added Smith," that it was somebody who was rather pleased with their handiwork and looked forward to the publicity surrounding the case."

"Could be. Oh here, I made you a copy of both sets of photos," said Dr. Marshall handing over a manila envelope.

Back at the office Jones waited impatiently for Constable Atkinson to return from his errand. Atkinson was visiting each bank and Post Office near Blount's flat to see if he had an account with them. Jones was experienced enough to know that many cases are solved due to the investigating team tracing the money trail left either by the victim or the killer. Everybody at the station was well aware of Blount's reputation, but it seems that nobody knew what Blount was up to after he left the force and Jones was hoping that Blount's finances would give them some clue as to where his money was coming from and eventually lead them to his killer. Constable Atkinson peered around Jones's open door.

" Can I come in sir?"

"Yes of course. I'll just call the Sgt. Ah, Smith just in time to hear. Carry on Constable."

"Well sir it's not really very good news. I tried Lloyds and Barclay's on Western Road; both are in walking distance from Blount's flat. No luck there. Then I tried the other Lloyd's along by Sackville Road and the Barclay's by Grand Avenue but nothing there either. Then I tried three Post Offices; Western Road, by Brunswick Square, then top of George Street, he could have walked through Hove Rec. to that one and finally the P.O. at the Seven Dials. Nothing at all. I showed them his photo, but no one seemed to know him. Sorry sir," said the Constable obviously disappointed at not being able to find anything.

"While I think about other means of finding Blount's accounts go down to the canteen for some well-earned lunch and report back later." Jones said, also disappointed that nothing turned up.

"It looks as though we'll have to go back to his flat and search more thoroughly. Even if it isn't his furniture everything must be taken apart as there has to be something we've missed. Files, records, papers of any kind, probably secreted away somewhere we would never think to look. So, this time everything is looked at until we find some evidence. Set that up Jack for about four o'clock this afternoon. Thanks."

Just as Smith was leaving Masters arrived at the door, he was grinning from ear to ear.

"Sir," he said to Jones as Smith hovered in the doorway. "You'll love this. We found how the body, or body parts, were moved around," Masters paused.

"Get on with it then," said a smiling Jones.

"We found a doorway in the summerhouse; it was behind a set of shelves full of garden pots and things. Anyway, we dragged it open and there were steps leading down to an underground cellar, then another passageway that came up behind the pantry in the kitchen. In the cellar we found an old wheelbarrow that looked as though it had bloodstains on it, anyways we bought it in for the lab boys to have a closer look."

Jones grinned across at Masters.

"You enjoyed that didn't you?"

"Yes sir, it's not often that I find an important clue."

"Well done. Once we confirm that the stain is Blount's blood then we'll know that the killer had an intimate knowledge of Baxter House and leaving the body there was not just convenience but a deliberate act. Constable let Dr. Marshall know about the wheelbarrow he would probably like to examine it too. Sgt. Smith is organizing a team to do a more thorough search of Blount's flat in Church Road starting at four o'clock. Be ready."

"Yes sir," was the eager reply

"Jack, I heard that the A.C.C. has plans to make changes to our reporting system have you heard anything yet?" asked Jones.

"No sir, nothing yet. I had heard that he was chasing up some of the uniform constables about the state of their monthly reports. But he hasn't talked to any of our men yet."

"Well we must keep on top of whatever he is up to, let me know if you hear anything, anything at all."

CHAPTER FOUR

Jones had called ahead to warn the manager of Blount's flat that they would be at the building at four o'clock, with a warrant to search Flat 6a, and that he expected full cooperation. When the cars pulled up in the forecourt of the building the manager ran out waving his arms.

"You cannot park there," he called. "Please park around the back. Our residents will be most upset to see these," pointing to the three police cars, "When they return. Please Inspector move them."

Hollingsworth was hopping around from foot to foot looking positively stricken, as he pleaded with Jones for his building's reputation. Jones nodded at Smith who signalled to the drivers to pull the cars around to the back parking area. The manager was almost grovelling as he thanked Jones, but Jones wanted more.   "Now it's your turn to cooperate. I give you my word that we will not damage any items that belong to you, but we must have privacy to conduct our search."

"But that's against our rules, other than the tenant; no one can go in without my presence. Absolutely not!"

Jones turned to his Sgt. "You know Sgt. I think it would be more convenient to have our cars at the front "

"Oh, very well, as long as I have your word Inspector," conceded the man and flounced away into the building.

Reaching Flat 6a Mr. Hollingsworth again explained the management policy but Jones remained adamant. They could hear the manager's peevish whine echoing down the corridor until the lift doors quietly closed off the man's voice.

The flat was furnished in a manner which portrayed wealth but also utilitarianism. There were few pictures on the walls, no personal photographs and no plants. An enormous black leather sofa and its matching armchair dominated the main room. One small glass-topped table held travel magazines whilst its partner on the other side of the sofa held a black telephone. The long curtains were richly embossed cream velvet edged with a black fringe. The luxurious oval carpet was a matching cream patterned with black circles. The bedroom was luxurious yet spartan, a large bed, one large black wardrobe and one man's chest of drawers. The only personal effects were the clothes hanging in the wardrobe. Four suits carrying labels of a London bespoke tailor, one Harris Tweed hacking jacket and three pairs of shoes, two black one brown, all leather.

"There's not much living done in this flat, it's such a bare and cold place to spent one's life," remarked Smith. He spoke to his men,

"You know the drill. You must be thorough but no breakages. We are looking for concealed paper records, account books, keys and things, so they could be hidden in very small places. Don't forget to put everything back as you found it, we don't want any problems with the management."

Jones walked across the room; he had spotted the corner of a brown attaché case poking out from behind the long curtains. He knew from experience that many, men especially, kept their important papers in such a case. But it was locked, and no amount of wiggling or thumping would spring the locks. Frustrated he was ready to use a knife on the locks when he heard a yell.

"Sir look at this. I found it in that small milk jug in the kitchen cupboard," explained Masters.

It was a small key, small enough to fit the locks on the case that Jones was still holding. Hopefully he tried the key in the lock and instantly the locks sprang open. Carrying the case over to the table Jones began a careful search of its contents. There were the usual Tenant's Agreement and a bundle of receipts for rent paid, always in cash as Mr. Hollingsworth had said, but neither a bankbook nor a savings book. In one of the compartments in the lid Jones found an envelope that contained yet another key. But this one was larger, more like an industrial padlock key than a house key.

"What do you think it is sir?" asked Smith looking over Jones's shoulder.

"Well it looks to me more like a garage or lock up or some kind of storage container. Perhaps that is why we cannot find anything here, he has it stashed in a locker or something."

"Look" said Jones moments later. Turning the key back and forth to catch the light.

"Here, I can just make out faint traces of a name. We'll take it back and get Forensic to clean it up and perhaps get a clearer look at the letters."

Each of the officers had completed their individual searches but had little to report. Every room had been given a thorough going over and then put back as it was. Even Smith had to admit the boys had done a neat job but still there was nothing to indicate what Blount was up to or where his wealth had come from. The only item of use was the key. Before they left the flat Smith double-checked every room and then locking the door, he followed Jones down the corridor into the lift.

"We are going to see our friend, the manager," Jones grinned at Smith, "I want to check out that application form that Blount produced when he took this flat. It seems strange to me that a Supt. who had been involved in Blount's leaving the force would actually sign a reference for him, under a different name and especially to a place like this." Smith knocked respectfully on the manager's door.

"Yes, yes what is it now? I thought you were done upstairs?" was the petulant response.

"Yes, we are, and the other officers have left your building, but I still have a couple of questions for you. First of all, did Mr. Ford have a car and is it here in the parking lot?"

"Oh yes. Mr. Ford had recently purchased a new Hillman Minx, it's there in his parking space, number fifteen on the lower parking. I have been keeping an eye on it until Mr. Ford returns." the manager proudly announced.

"Well I will be sending an official towing truck to collect it tomorrow, for examination." Jones stated. A deflated Hollingsworth sat back down at his large, ornate desk.

"Well what else do you want?" he asked grudgingly.

"I would like to see both the application form and the letter of reference that your Mr. Ford gave you when he took this flat. Before you object, remember I do have a warrant."

Retrieving a small key from the pocket of his silk waistcoat the manager opened his file draw, took out a blue folder and reluctantly handed it over to Jones. Searching through Jones suddenly handed a paper to Smith.

"What about this? Is this correct?" Smith peered at the paper.

"I knew Supt. McLeod for many years, and this is nothing like his signature."

"Well Mr. Hollingsworth it looks as though your Mr. Ford was not so respectable after all, you were fooled by a forgery. Good afternoon."

They left the office, leaving Mr. Hollingsworth gasping for words.

CHAPTER FIVE

The next day Jones, Smith and a team of uniformed officers returned to Steyning to conduct a house-to-house survey of the houses in the vicinity of the Baxter house. Jones stopped by at the estate agents in Steyning to pick up the house key.

"Good morning Miss Wilcott," said Jones, "I would like to have the key to the Baxter house as we have to re- check some of our original notes." Phyllis drew the key out of her drawer.

"Here we are Inspector." Phyllis said handing Jones the heavy key, "anything else I can help you with?"

"Well there is something actually. Did you or Mr. Trent know that there is an underground passage linking the summerhouse to the kitchen in the main house?"

"Oh, no I have never heard of that. Just a minute let me check my listings." She grabbed a small pile of papers and started to flip quickly through the pages. "Here it is. No, there is nothing mentioned here about anything like that." she began to straighten up the papers, "do you think that was where um, it- was done?"

"We're not sure yet but that is the main reason for our return today. Have you thought of anything that might help us in our investigation? "

"Not really," she said "but I did look up the details of the last tenant. They were the first tenants after old Mr. Pope died. A Mr. and Mrs. Fletcher, they lived there for about four years before moving out to Australia. Unfortunately, we do not have an address for them."

"Did they have any family?"

"I had heard that there was a son. Probably be in his early twenties by now, I expect the neighbours will know more, sorry."

"What about further back in Mr. Pope's time, do you know of anybody who worked for him up at the house like a gardener or housekeeper?"

"No, our records do not show anybody else's name but probably Mr. Siddely the solicitor would know more. Sorry"

"No that's good you have been very helpful. Can I keep the key for a few days?"

"Certainly, I'm in no hurry to go back there again."

Jones seemed to have more questions as he hovered around her desk but then abruptly said "Goodbye" and quickly turned to leave the office. As the door shut Stella abruptly went into the kitchen area making strange noises into her handkerchief. Phyllis followed her in.

"What's in the world is the matter with you?"

"Oh Phyllis, you are so naive he was chatting you up." Phyllis blushed.

"No, you are mistaken."

"I am not just you wait and see," retorted Stella.

While Jones was in Trent's office Smith had been in contact with Masters confirming that the uniformed officers had started their house-to house search...

"All seems to be going well." Smith reported to Jones. "The village is quite spread out so three of the men are going down the main High Street talking to the shopkeepers. Two others have taken the car and are working their way to those houses that are isolated from the village but close to the Baxter House. I asked them all to be back at the main house by three o'clock."

"Good," said Jones, "what do you know about Steyning?"

"Quite an interesting place this. The church is the oldest building established about mid-fourteenth century. Then a small community grew up around the church, mostly farmers really. But because it was on the way to Shoreham and its harbour it also became a favourite stop for travellers. There are still a few of the old pubs and inns left on the High Street. In the thirties it was a very popular place for artists and craftsman. I expect the land was cheap then and there was plenty of it around here, so they built large studios and later opened galleries to sell their own work."

"I imagine that these days the inhabitants are a close-knit group and value their privacy above all else."

"Yes, and there are many such places through Mid-Sussex. Places where one has to live for at least fifty years before you are accepted as a true member of the village community." The two men sat in a companiable silence. They both knew places just like that and knew the difficulties that police encountered when investigations were necessary.

"How did you get on at Trent's?" asked Smith.

"Well nothing was known about a secret passage, but Miss Wilcott did give me some information about the last tenants. They went to Australia, but they did have a son who is in his early twenties, who stayed here. We have to contact the solicitor, Mr. Siddely, to see if he knows the boy's whereabouts. We need to make contact with him as, like all young people, he would have thoroughly explored the house and grounds."

Masters was waiting at the house for them and quickly guided them around the back to the summerhouse and then down through the underground passageway to the door at the end, which opened into the scullery section of the kitchen.

"What have you found out about this?" Jones asked.

"Sir, it looks as though the doors are in good shape and the locks work, not even stiff, and these large hinges have been oiled recently. There are some wheel marks running through the passage, probably made by the wheelbarrow as the wheels have metal rims. In the scullery there's a large table that has lots of cuts and gouges in it. Perhaps that's where he was… you know sir, cut up?"

"Or perhaps," chuckled Smith "it is simply where they butchered their animals ready for storing. Remember, originally this was a farm."

"I know Sarge, but it fits doesn't it?"

"Yes, it does," agreed Jones, "but let's not get carried away, let's find a few more facts before we talk in absolutes. I would like you to go around the outside of the house again and thoroughly check all windows and doors for any sign of forced entry, look for footprints on sills etc. in fact everywhere and thoroughly check the summerhouse for a weapon or any poison. I know you did it once but with more evidence we need to look again." said Jones.

Masters strode off on his assignment, but Jones knew by the young officer's body language that he was not happy with his Inspector. Jones chuckled to Smith, "That young man reminds me of me when I first started, very impulsive, jumping to conclusions and thinking that anybody over twenty was slow. My impulsiveness did get me into trouble when I made an accusation that was later proved to be utterly wrong. I felt like a fool but my Sgt. was patient with me and I did learn to curb my impatience and wait for all the evidence before coming to a decision."

"I'll talk to him," said Smith "At least he does listen to me. I'll sort him out, he's a good lad and very keen to do well." Although the two officers took another walk through each of the rooms, they found nothing new but were pleased to see that the forensic team had left the rooms in order.

Coming down the central staircase they found that most of the survey team had returned and were waiting in the entrance for their orders. Jones indicated the dining room where they again sat around the large oval table. Jones started "All I need at this moment is any information given to you that you found surprising, interesting or strange."

A young constable spoke up,

"Sir, some of the elderly people close by remembered the original owner, a Mr. Pope, they said that once his wife died, he became a recluse and didn't go out or allow any work to be done on the property. Apparently, some local farmers wanted to rent the pastureland for their cattle, but he wouldn't even answer the door to them."

"Anything mentioned about a housekeeper or cleaning person who went into the house?"

"No Sir," was the chorused answer.

"The village kids wouldn't even go scrumping in the small orchard, they were so afraid of the man," said another voice.

"What about the next people who lived there?" Smith asked.

"Apparently their closest neighbour, a Mrs. Nash, said that they were fine and quite friendly but that their son was a horrible, spoilt brat, who was rude to everyone and did get into trouble with the police from time to time."

"Anyone else get more information on the son?"

"Yes, he was in trouble for breaking windows and stealing stuff out of people's gardens."

"Do we have a name and whereabouts?"

36

"Their name was Fletcher, but his name is Stuart Hughes and Mrs. Nash was sure that he had been back to the house during the past year. It was in April she thought, she was out walking her dog and saw Hughes near the summerhouse."

"Thank you. That information will help us move along. Please have your full notes into Sgt. Smith by lunchtime tomorrow. We are finished now so you can return to Brighton."

Constable Masters was helping Smith replace the dustsheets. he was smiling "That's sounds promising Sarge I didn't find anything else outside but on closer inspection the summerhouse floor is cleaner than I would have expected and the scullery floor has only our muddy footprints which is strange considering it has been empty for so long. I took a sample of something reddish from between the floor tiles I'll get it to the forensics when I get back to the office."

"Well done," said Smith.

Once back in Brighton Jones decided to drop in at The Castle on his way home to his flat. Since being appointed to the Sussex Constabulary Jones had made a point of visiting many of the pubs that were dotted around the centre of Brighton and Hove. As all good policemen knew pubs were the social centres of any community. Of course, not all citizens went to pubs but those that did were usually the citizens that most interested the police for they knew most about what was happening in their particular neighbourhood. Sometimes they were old lags who had done their time but always returned to their old haunts. Sometimes they were men who just skirted the law but always knew what deals were about to be made and could be helpful to the police when they felt like it. 'Shady' Lane was such a man and he and Jones had struck up an acquaintance soon after Jones first visited The Castle. Each knew what the other was about, but Jones liked the little man and enjoyed his company and his outrageous anecdotes.

Lane was born in London at the turn of the century. "My old mum was named Miranda and she was a chorus girl who worked in the London and provincial theatres. Even did a year or two at the Windmill so she said. But I never knew my father. Mum always said that he was some aristocrat naval officer who was her lover for a month and then went back to sea and she never saw him again. Perhaps that's why she called me Horatio Fisher Lane; she said they were naval heroes."

Horatio was short, thin and moved with quick jerky actions. Although never in serious trouble with the law, Lane liked to project the image of his being in the game, one of the boys. He always wore a sports jacket of the brightest checks accompanied by brightly coloured shirts with an equally bright bowtie. His trousers were usually a check material but bearing no likeness to his jacket. A pair of two-tone shoes and paisley socks would complete his attire. But he had adopted a unique accessory for he was never seen without a green, eyeshade which was perched high on his forehead. His friends often teased him about going to bed with it on and it was this attachment that led to his nickname of Shady Lane.

Jones had soon realized that this rather unusual character knew just about everything that was going on in town. He professed to know, on a personal level, every dealer, every gambler and every bookie within a twenty-mile radius of Brighton. He said he knew all the crooked trainers, the con men who worked on the piers and the beach and of course he knew every policeman in the Sussex Constabulary. Jones had some doubts about Shady's final claim but this afternoon he was headed towards The Castle to put that claim to the test. He was determined to bring the conversation around to past officers and see what the little man knew about ex-Sgt Ray Blount.

"Afternoon Inspector, 'ad a busy day?" asked Shady as Jones made himself comfortable on the neighbouring barstool.

"Usual stuff Shady, as you know it never ends. What'll you have?"

"A pint of bitter please gov."

"Did you watch the Albion game on Saturday?"

"Yer, what a waste of me money. They played like a bunch of women, kept falling down as soon as the ball came near them. No wonder they stay down in the Third Division."

"Do you ever go to London to watch any of those teams?"

"I bin to watch Chelsea a few times. Their grounds are near where me mum and I lived when I was young. Do you watch football Mr. Jones?"

"Yes, I watch football and rugby when I can."

"Not much rugby around these parts. Do you go up to the Smoke to see games?"

"Occasionally. I meet up with an old army buddy of mine. We have a meal and then go on to the game. I often go out to local club games, some are really good," added Jones

They sipped contentedly on their beer just watching the other customers come and go. They were in no hurry to finish. It was what Shady referred to as the 'in between hour'. The after-work drinkers had slipped in for a quick one before going home for dinner while it was much too early for the serious evening drinkers to arrive.

"Shady you said to me some time ago that you knew all the Sussex policeman, both past and present, is that true?"

"Yes, you give me a copper's name and I'll tell you about 'im, or 'er too these days."

"Sgt. Ray Blount."

"You mean ex-Sgt. Blount. 'e was a bad lot. I always made sure to stay out of 'is way. He frightened me, 'e was a big man who used his size to bully people. It didn't matter who you were you either did a deal with him or 'e beat you up. At least he sent his mates to beat you up. Good job they got rid of him."

"What sort of deals was he looking for?"

"Sometimes he asked shopkeepers for protection money, especially those whose shops were damaged by the bombings. 'E would be on their doorsteps within hours, the smoke hardly cleared away, saying that he would protect them from looters if they paid 'im money."

"Did he protect them?"

"Well sometimes those that didn't pay had their shops broken into and things went missing. Nobody could prove anything, but it was after the war and there were lots of bigger things for the police to worry about then. Sometimes if he caught people without their blackouts drawn properly, he would ask for money not to report them. Lots of things like that. I guess some of your lot finally got enough guts to kick 'im out. Why you asking? summat 'appened to 'im?"

"I can't say just now, but thanks. Do you want another?" asked Jones pointing at Shady's almost empty glass.

"No thanks mate, I'm fine. Just nursing this one. If you want to know more about Blount go visit the pubs on Upper James St. The Great Globe was one of his hangouts and try the Hand in Hand that was up there too. Some of the locals will be bound to remember him he wasn't liked, just put up with being as 'e was a copper."

Shady lifted his glass as Jones made ready to leave.

"If Blount 'as gone I say good riddance to bad rubbish. Lots o' people will be glad to see the back of that one." Shady lifted his glass in a farewell gesture as Jones left.

CHAPTER SIX

First thing in the morning Jones went to see his Supt to update him on the investigation.

"What on earth was he doing to manage to live in a place like that?" asked the very puzzled Young.

"To my knowledge there were no rich relatives in Blount's family." answered Jones.   "Then I'm afraid that given his personality and the problems he got himself into I believe that he must have been getting his money by some sort of illegal activities; he was that kind of man I'm sorry to say. What about the house at Steyning, any leads out there?" asked Young.

"Not yet Sir, but we are tracking down the son of the former tenants who had a reputation of being wild and was often in trouble, and being a boy was bound to know about the underground passage. He was even seen out there this spring."

"Okay thanks, just keep me informed. You know this is going to reflect so badly on our department. He was one of ours, yet nobody seemed to have any idea what he was up to. I know we were continually short staffed during those years, but he should never have been allowed to get away with so much. Now you and I are going to have to bear the brunt of the criticism," complained the worried man.

"Yes sir, but we'll get through it. Anything new from the ACC yet?"

"Nothing official yet Dai but he has called for a review on all reporting procedures both internal and external. I know he has the office in a real turmoil and the Chief Constable seems oblivious to the upset this is causing."

Jones had a great deal of respect for his senior officer. Jones felt Young treated all the officers fairly and compassionately. Young encouraged individual initiative while maintaining a very public respect for the Rules and Regulations handed down by the Home Office. He listened attentively to suggestions offered, and most importantly if things ever went wrong, he was always loyal to his men as long as they had acted properly.
Smith was waiting for Jones.

"I am sending WPC Jenkins down to Archives to go through all Blount's reports and logbooks stored there. Let's see what he has left behind. Then Masters has started to track down Stuart Hughes. If he was at the house then he would have had a car at some time and Motor records would have his registration," finished Smith

"If you don't mind Sgt. I want Masters to do something else. Last evening, I had a most interesting conversation with Shady Lane, and he gave me Blount's favourite pubs, where according to Shady's sources, Blount spent most of his off-duty time. Send Masters over there to see what he can find out, especially about Blount's last three years. Give the Stuart Hughes assignment to another officer."

"Okay will do. Anything else sir?"

"Yes, you and I are going over to North Street to Brown's the locksmith. I'm very anxious to see where this key of Blount's belongs, and I've heard that Brown is the best in town."

Mr. Brown lived up to his reputation and after thoroughly cleaning the key and putting it under the microscope he was able to discern the maker's name from one side and three of the five figures on the other side.

"It's a Rogers's key for a large padlock. I do know Hove Council gives out these kinds of padlocks and keys to people who rent their small garages and lockups. If you went to the engineer at Hove Town hall, he could tell by these numbers what area of town these places are, the numbers I can read would give you the actual street and number of the garage. Try that Inspector."

"Jack would you follow that up? I'm going back. It's getting close to opening time and I want to speak to Masters about his assignment."

By the time Jones had sent Masters off with his instructions Smith was back with news of the key.

"Apparently it is one of a series that were handed out for the council garages at the back of Sackville Road Hove. The missing numbers were actually letters; S.R. standing for Sackville Road and the number 272 denoted garage number 72 in row 2. The garage had been rented by a Mr. Ford and he was first issued with the key a couple of years ago and is fully paid up for this year. There were two keys issued to each renter. I have a map of the Sackville Road garages, and he did warn me that the entrance is so small it's very easy to miss."

"Okay let's go and see what we can find at Sackville Road," said Jones as he gathered up his coat.

Once through the narrow entrance the men could see the four rows of identical garages, each just large enough for one car, in an area surrounded by high industrial buildings. There was barely enough room to drive the car between the rows of garages and it would take a very skilled driver to get a car inside one of the centre spots. They parked at the end of the back row and walked the few steps across to Number 72.

"Let's give it a try," said Jones. The key turned smoothly in the padlock and Smith easily swung open the doors to reveal a very expensive, silver convertible sports car.

"What do we have here? Your former colleague certainly had a lifestyle far beyond that of an ordinary ex-copper."

Smith was amazed. "Wait 'til the lads back at the station hear about this. Not only does he have a new Hillman back at his flat, but he had this one as well."

"But what is even more interesting is that although he was found in Steyning his one car is still in the parking garage at his flat and now a second car is still here, so how did he get to Steyning? I can't see a man like this travelling on the bus and look the key is still in the lock. You go back and summon the garage to send along someone to move this car while I look in those cabinets back there," directed Jones.

Along the back wall of the garage were three large metal filing cabinets. Each of the filing cabinets was locked but Jones soon located the key to the first one hanging at the back. The top drawer was full of photos of a woman, presumably his wife, with children and some documents relating to purchases. The second drawer was full of car magazines. Nothing much in the bottom drawer just some wartime souvenirs. But Jones spotted another key hanging just inside the top drawer and that key opened the next cabinet. In the top drawer of that one were about thirty file folders, no names were visible, just a series of numbers and letters with either a black tab or a brown one. In the second drawer they found a neatly folded police uniform, complete with cap, the boots were in the lower drawer.

"Must have kept this for a reason" said Smith "seeing the uniform." Using the next key, they opened the third cabinet in which were a series of manila envelopes containing what appeared to be legal papers.

"At last something! We need to get all of this taken into Brighton," said Jones. "We'll take all the files and the envelopes with us and leave the uniform and everything else for the officers to bring along later," said Jones.

"Well I certainly cannot get the truck in here," said the mechanic, joining Jones and Smith at the garage doorway.

"The key is in the lock," said Smith "so you can drive it out to the truck to hitch up."

"What idiot would leave the key in this kind of car, just inviting trouble? Must have more money than sense if you ask me? But driving this will be a pleasure Sir," said the smiling mechanic as he slid himself into the driving seat of the silver car and started the engine. Once Blount's car had gone Jones and Smith piled all the files and envelopes into the back seat of their car and headed for the station.

Jenkins was at Jones's door as soon as she heard their voices in the corridor. She came in carrying a case box full of beige file folders. Both Jones and Smith looked up.

"Well constable anything informative in that box?"

"Sir, as you know as each case is closed all the relevant materials and legal documents are filed away with the investigating officer's signature on the box. The officer also had to fill in the appropriate forms that signified the date of closing and the resolution. These forms were placed in the Master File in the superintendent's office for approximately three years, after which they were sent to archives to be stored separately from the case boxes."

"Yes, go on," said Jones

"There are some oddities, or perhaps missing papers would be a better description as some of these case files are empty. The information on the tabs that identify the cases have
been scratched out leaving no way to identify the case. When I checked on Blount's name in the Master File Record Book there were some under

his name but there were other entries where I could make out the 'B' for Blount but the rest had been obliterated by some kind of ink eraser," explained Jenkins. "I did check the number of empty files with the numbers of missing details in the Master record Book and the numbers do match."

"Were you able to match up the case boxes with the remaining entries?" asked Jones.

"Yes, they are all matched."

"So, perhaps the missing reports are cases where no charges were actually laid," said Jones,

"But even when charges are not laid there should be a report of the investigation and the conclusion reached."

"Constable would you stay here and using these files that we found in Blount's garage see if you can find any connection between them and the crossed-out ones in the Master file. I don't want those files to leave my office."

Jones and Smith walked down the corridor towards the canteen.

"I wonder why he would want to blank out and then steal case files. He had to have used them to work out some scheme that would benefit him financially. Perhaps he took his protection racket to a higher level?" wondered Jones.

"Do you mean blackmail?" said Smith.

"Why not? He certainly had the means to get any information he needed, and he had the authority of the uniform to intimidate. And you say he was a big man, bad tempered as well. Sounds like he had the means and the power, and if things weren't going well for him here, the motivation to go into business for himself would be that much greater."

"It will be interesting to see what Jenkins can pull out of those files, but it certainly doesn't look good for us as a police force to have one of ours turn out such a bad apple," conceded Smith.

CHAPTER SEVEN

It was a bright, sunny Monday morning with just a hint of a breeze gently stirring the leaves. The Jaguar purred to a halt at the tall iron gates where the chauffeur waited for the guard to walk out and swing the gates open and then he drove the car sedately around the pebbled circular drive to pull up at the double front doors. The house was vast, and the imposing front façade was indicative of the luxury that lay behind. The entrance was an enormous double oak door which was set back behind four white Romanesque pillars which stretched across the driveway creating a portico for the car. The windows were many with their small leaded panes holding ornate stained-glass panels. The house itself was protected from the gaze of passers-by by a stand of tall spruce trees along the outer wall and then shorter but thicker willows that lined the driveway.   Waiting at the top of the pristine steps, in her gray dress, white nurses' cap, and wearing her habitual smile, was Matron. The chauffeur opened his door and walked around to open the back passenger door. As a portly gentleman eased himself out of the car door Matron sang out her usual.

"Good morning Sir."

"Good morning Matron and how are things this morning? No concerns I hope," boomed the voice from behind the beard as the portly man climbed the steps.

"Oh no Mr. Crandall there is nothing amiss. The surgery is ready for your ten and eleven o'clock appointments and the two new surgical patients arrived last evening and had a comfortable night. Mr. Brown, Mr. Green and Mr. Black each had a comfortable night and are following their medical regime very conscientiously. Unfortunately, Mrs. Daisy is experiencing great pain after yesterday's surgery and the two patients in the special rooms are moving into stage two of their treatment. They have been quite noisy and were disturbing others but did settle down after taking their medication."

By now the pair had reached the man's office, the surgeon just slightly ahead of a rather breathless matron.   He continued to smile as Matron droned on through her report. He enjoyed hearing the patients referred to with their assumed names. It was his idea to give the female clients names of flowers and the male clients were known by colours. He felt that this was just a small part of securing their anonymity while they were at his clinic.

"Thank you Matron I will meet with you at nine sharp for Rounds."

With that he walked into his office, firmly closing the door on Matron.

There was nothing Sir Michael Crandall, Surgeon enjoyed more than walking into his own hospital, being greeted by his subservient Matron and practicing his medical skills on those who had enough money to pay for the very best. But this morning he deliberately ignored the papers on his desk, he had other more worrying concerns on his mind that needed to be resolved very soon and he could only think them through in the privacy of his office.

Crandall had first established his practice in London where his clientele consisted of established actors and actresses as well as those members of the aristocracy who needed special help. It didn't take long for Crandall's name and reputation for both privacy and excellent care, to spread amongst the widening entertainment world. His practice grew that he needed a separate and more private location to accommodate those patients who needed more than just a visit to his rooms in Harley Street. Hove was well known for its clean and bracing sea air and as he had an elderly aunt already living there, he decided to base his new clinic in that area. Besides through his London practice he already had many connections to Brighton's growing theatre-world.

Dyke Road was a wide, majestic road that coursed its way from the Seven Dials up to the beginning of the Downs following the boundary line between Brighton and Hove. It wasn't a busy road, just a bus every half-hour and local car owners. The Hove side of Dyke Road was a considered prestigious location, well suited for the more affluent citizens and the large, set back, houses were owned by London financiers, by barristers and some owners of the larger shops in town. Crandall had purchased the land, drawn up his own plans and opened his hospital ten years ago. He also moved his private home down to Hove going to his London practice, only on Wednesdays and Thursdays.

Over the year's success had bought more recognition and the conferring of a knighthood served to increase Sir Michael Crandall's clientele and his already high opinion of his own importance. Only one issue marred the doctor's life and that involved the unfortunate death of a beautiful, talented, actress while undergoing a procedure at his clinic. Officially, the young lady's death was attributed to pneumonia and she was quietly buried in the cemetery near her parent's home. Unfortunately for Sir Michael her family was not satisfied with his explanation and her brother went to the local police to make known his concern. Although the local police did make an initial visit to the clinic Crandall was very confident that the brother of the young woman had no actual proof of any wrongdoing by the medical team. Secondly, he played the doctor/patient confidentiality card, which was always a stumbling block for official enquiries.

All was quiet for a few weeks and then, one evening, the investigating officer turned up on the doorstep of Crandall's home. Crandall was furious and was not prepared to let the officer into his private home. He shut the door and went to call the Chief Constable, but the policeman let himself in and followed Crandall to his office.

"Get out of here. I certainly did not invite you into my home. You will hear about this. Now get out."   But Blount had his foot against the door and leaned forward in a very threatening manner,

"Before you talk to the C.C, I would advise you to listen to what I have to say. I warn you now if you continue your telephone call you will regret it." Crandall was speechless. Nobody spoke to him in this manner. He would not put up with it. He slammed down the telephone and strode across to other man.

"Now look here my good man" he began but then Blount grabbed Crandall's arms and dumped him unceremoniously into one of his own Queen Anne chairs.

"Listen mate I am not your good man and never will be. Just sit still and listen very carefully to what I have to say."

Crandall succumbed. He really did not want to antagonize this large, powerful man who towered over him by at least ten inches. All he wanted was for him to leave but Crandall was frightened by the aggressive tone of his visitor and felt he had no option but to calmly listen and try to keep his fear hidden. Blount drew up another chair in front of Crandall and sat so close that the men's knees touched. Crandall squirmed at this proximity and Blount laughed at his victim's reaction.

"Since my official visit to your clinic I have been keeping an eye on the comings and goings up there on Dyke Road. Despite your security, it is quite easy to get in close enough to your front door to identify some of your visitors, or should I say patients?"

Crandall was still indignant,

"I'll report you for this. My friend the Chief Constable will soon put a stop to your spying on me."

"No, he will not," Blount stated, with his face even closer to Crandall's. "Not once I have told him what is really going on in your clinic."

"What do you mean?" but the doctor's courage was fading fast as he grew more fearful of what Blount was going to say next.

"A very interesting lot I would say. Well known society figures, some of whom are known to have problems with alcohol or in some cases are suspected of having a preference for opium. Some are highly placed government officials who are publicly said to be on sick leave. But the most interesting group of all are the young girls, some of them daughters of respectable families others who are known actresses, who stay at the clinic for private surgical procedures." Blount smiled knowingly as he spoke the last few words. "As a doctor you know what you are doing is illegal and should you be found out you would be struck off the Medical List."

Crandall found some courage.

"You have no idea what I do in my clinic. You are just making assumptions based on poor information." Crandall left his seat and moved quickly to the door.

"Now get out of my house you insolent creature."

He flung open the door, but Blount was not so easily put off.

"I do have solid evidence against you, and I have someone willing to testify in court."

Crandall moaned. He wasn't entirely convinced that Blount had any hard evidence against him, but could he afford to call Blount's bluff?

"What do you want me to do?" he asked quietly.

"Just pay up and nobody else will ever find out."

"How much?"

"Not a lot, to you anyway, just three hundred pounds a month. It must be in cash and you will pass it over to me at a place of my choice. The money must not be withdrawn separately from your bank. I don't want some nosey parker of a bank manager asking you questions about a regular withdrawal."

The monthly payments began that night and the doctor had continued to pay up for the past five years. He needed silence to protect his patients and so protect his very lucrative practice. Unfortunately for him his secret had been found out by an individual who had the power and authority to bring Crandall's life crumbling down in ruins, to destroy everything that Crandall had built, including his reputation and quite possibly his son's marriage to the daughter of an influential Minister of the Crown.

Recently Crandall had decided to put an end to Blount and his blackmail scheme. He was not going to be bullied anymore by this monster. He, Crandall, was going to end this torture once and for all. Last evening at home he had devised a plan that would protect his practice, his reputation and his family while putting an end to Officer Blount and today he would put his plan in motion. He lifted the telephone and used his private line to make the one telephone call that would free him. He looked around his spacious office fully confident that by the time he retired for the night his worries would be over. As his finished his call a sedate knock on his office door signalled Matron's arrival. Rising from his chair he tugged at the points of his waistcoat confident that this latest decision would keep all that he possessed safe.

CHAPTER EIGHT

Inspector Jones was becoming frustrated at the length of time it was taking to decipher the codes on Blount's files. He had learned a great deal about the late Sgt. Blount but nothing that really related to his death or his secret files. Reading every paper in Blount's Employment file. He learned that Blount had been with the Sussex Constabulary for five years, having transferred down south from Newcastle. When he first arrived at Brighton all seemed to be well as he and his wife Edna and their two young girls soon settled into their new community. He appeared to be well liked at the station and nothing negative had been reported in his earlier file from Newcastle. There were a couple of performance assessments that mentioned Blount had a tendency to be impatient with citizens who wanted to lay complaints and one mentioned that Blount had a quick temper. But all had seemed well, that is until the one summer.

This report, found tucked at the back of the other records, was an account of a conversation between two officers from Sussex, who were up in Newcastle doing a course, with two officers from the Newcastle station. They stated, in their own handwriting that when they were in Newcastle, they had mentioned that Ray Blount had settled well into the Sussex force and that he and his family seemed to be very happy in Brighton. At first their Newcastle colleagues had been reluctant to say much about Blount but as they became more comfortable with the men from Brighton, they explained exactly why Ray Blount had moved south.

"He got himself in a jam," one officer had said.

"He was a bully to junior officers and treated woman, both at the station and those needing assistance, very rudely," said the other.

According to the Newcastle men Blount had allowed his bad temper and his bias against women and foreigners of any kind to colour his judgment when dealing with cases involving such individuals and finally, after a particularly abusive outburst, Blount's Superintendent had told him to transfer to another station far away or resign altogether from the police force. The report finished with a comment from both of the Sussex officers that until then they had not heard of any negative report of Blount's work.

Jones's next option was to examine any files that Supt. McLeod had left behind when he retired. It was there that Jones found more evidence of Blount's misconduct. The first serious negative report appeared about six months after Blount was involved in the chase of a burglar who eventually fell through the glass roof of a building and was badly injured. The burglar claimed that Blount had hit him with his truncheon and then pushed him down into the glass. Although a second officer was present Blount was not accused of anything, but it was soon after that incident that some of his colleagues grew concerned about Blount's conduct. It was reported that he was rude to members of the public and that he was morose and short tempered with his colleagues. Gradually Blount became more and more ill-tempered and rumour was that he was physically abusing his wife Edna.

This was evidenced one day by a report recording that Edna Blount came in to speak privately to Blount's superior and the desk sergeant noticed her bruised face. The record shows that Blount was offered medical assistance and a leave of absence, but he refused all help stating that there was nothing wrong with him. Shortly after that a letter arrived addressed to Superintendent McLeod from Edna Blount saying that she couldn't stand Blount's bad temper anymore and she and her girls were on their way to Scotland to live with her brother.

From that time on Blount's record showed incidents of insubordination, assaulting detainees and being intoxicated on duty. Eventually after several disciplinary hearings Blount was fired from the Force for misconduct. By then he had few, if any, friends left. Even those who tried to help him by keeping in touch and offering odd jobs were eventually driven away by his ill temper. Within weeks it seemed that Blount simply disappeared into the mainstream of the population.

Constable Jenkins continued to puzzle over the codes used by Blount trying to find at least one common factor that would link the letters and numbers logically. It was a strange mix of numbers and letters with little visual consistency not appearing to have been arranged in any particular order. Jenkins's writing pad was covered in the same letters and numbers along with a multitude of arrows going to and fro the page as she endeavoured to make the linkage. She stood up at her desk, stretching when she caught a glimpse of the letters GWR in very large print on a poster. Suddenly she was inspired and with fresh paper she wrote out the first code DS194A. She knew that DA was repeated inside on the front page of Blount's copy and she made the assumption that those letters represented the initial of the person Blount was interviewing. Jenkins checked other files from Blount's cabinet and was able to match two letters in each to the files tab. At last she felt she was getting somewhere. Half an hour later she knocked at Jones's office door.

"Can I come in Sir?"

"Yes do. I hope you found something for me"

"I think so Sir, I have finally decoded these tabs r."

"Great. Show me"

"They appear to show the date of an incident and the initials of the person involved"

"How?"

"The first one is DS.194 A. The second letter is the month because he used both Ma and My representing March and May. Then he used Ja, Ju and Jy which could be January, June and July. For April he used Ap and then Au for August, everything else is single letters so S is September. The next two numbers represent the date as no number goes higher than 31 and the last number is the year as they only go from 1 to 4 and then he was gone from the force. So, DS 194 A says that a person with initials D.A became involved with Blount on September 19th in the first year of his scam. I double checked on the Master List and there's a scratching out between others listed for the 19th in that year."

"Well done Jenkins. Have you done all of the files?"

"I have done all of the tabs sir, now I'm working on the money lists. At least they appear to be money totals as they are all in the hundreds, to me they must represent some kind of payments. Also, the number listed beside them seems to have repeated dates as again the numbers do not go higher than 31. Some earlier numbers seem to have come to a stop. Look at this one marked DA like the file, well there are no more amounts recorded after this one so perhaps something happened to whoever was paying. Perhaps they died?"

"What do you think we are looking at Constable?"

"Blackmail. At least that's what it looks like to me, sir."

CHAPTER NINE

Ellen was so excited that her Monday morning bus ride to the town centre seemed to take hours rather than the actual twenty minutes. Her boss was in London attending Fashion Week and she, Ellen would be in charge of the shop for three whole days. All by herself. Nobody looking over her shoulder telling her what to do. She couldn't wait to get started.

Ellen loved her job. She enjoyed helping ladies choose a dress or blouse and had become quite practiced at knowing what style suited which lady. But she didn't like her boss Mrs. Ainslee, Ellen thought her rude and impatient with the tradesmen who came to the shop and sometimes even with the customers. Mrs. Ainslee knew her clientele well but had little time for the ladies who came into her store to try on dresses that she knew were way beyond their financial means.

"Why don't they go down to the shops the other end of the High Street? More their style?" She would sniff as she hung the unwanted dresses back on the rack. Madame Stephanie`s was the only Haute Couture salon in the small town of Lancing. It was located at the right end of the High Street and was surrounded by other high-class establishments. Next door was a Lineners that specialized in selling lace from Brussels and linen from Ireland. On the other side of Madame Stephanie`s was a haberdashery that imported special silks and ribbons from Europe and the Far East.

Ellen carefully took the backdoor key from her handbag and slid it into the lock. Once inside she switched off the burglar alarm then took off her coat and hat and hung them carefully on the hook behind the door. Then she pulled on the black cotton coat that Mrs. Ainslee demanded her assistants wear while they were out in the salon. Actually, it was a very stylish garment that had deep pockets to hold tape measures, pins etc. that every good fitter needed. Ellen checked her wristwatch; five minutes to nine o`clock, just time to have a quick look round to see that all was well. She walked past the fitting rooms, pulled across the curtains that led into the main salon and stopped dead in her tracks.

"Oh my God. What has happened, who did this?" she cried out.

The salon was a mess with empty, torn boxes strewn across the floor. Some of the chairs had been slashed and the two floor to ceiling mirrors were just pieces of broken glass spread over the floor. Ellen carefully stepped over the mess and pulled back the curtains behind which hung the most expensive dresses, but not today. Not one of the high-priced gowns was there, just a yawning empty space.

Ellen felt sick but she went straight to the telephone and dialled 999 and reported the burglary to the police. She did manage to get a message to Mrs. Àinslee in London and the owner arrived back at her salon in the late afternoon. By then the police had done their investigation and had left the unfortunate Ellen to wait for her boss. Mrs. Ainslee came storming in.

"You silly bitch; how did you let this happen?"

"It wasn't my fault Mrs. Ainslee. It was like this when I came in this morning. I have cleaned up the floor and put the broken glass outside for the dustman that's what the policeman told me to do."

"What, you called the police!"

"Well I called 999 to report the burglary and they turned up quite quickly," Ellen turned to her note pad and read out, "A Sgt. Blount and a Constable Waters."

"What did they say?"

"That they would put out a notice about the missing dresses and that they would be back out tomorrow or the next day to talk to you. They would like a general description of everything that is missing."

She strode up and down her salon wondering how to handle this situation. Unknown to Ellen Mrs. Ainslee had a good idea who had trashed her shop and why, but she wasn't about to tell her silly little assistant that. She knew she could replace her stock, but it was the involvement of the police that scared her. What if they dug around and found out something about her little scam? She would be had up for fraud and probably sent to prison.

"Oh no I can't let that happen," she spoke out loud.

"What was that Mrs. Ainslee?" asked Ellen, still hovering around trying to be useful.

"Nothing, just thinking out loud."

"I'm sorry that this happened Mrs. Ainslee. Is there anything else for me to do before I go home?"

"No, just go home. Come in at the same time tomorrow and we can do a check of what is missing and the costing.

Within a week Mrs. Ainslee had restocked her salon and it was business as usual. She had supplied the police with a reasonably close list of what was missing, although she had deliberately left off at least a dozen of her top line designer gowns. Ellen did not work on the list and was unaware of the missing details. By the end of the month Mrs. Ainslee felt secure that her little secret had not been discovered and began to restock her top designer labels.

Arriving at her home late one Friday evening she noticed a car parked very close to the entrance of her drive. She wondered for a moment whose it could be and then dismissed it as probably a breakdown. She drove into her garage, parked her car and walked across to the house.

"Mrs. Ainslee?" called a husky voice from the shadows of the trees.

"Yes, who are you what do you want?"

"I am Sgt. Blount and I want to talk to you about the burglary at your shop in the High Street. We didn't meet on the morning of the burglary."

"No. That's right we have never met before. But why this evening? Why didn't you come to the shop? Why are you here at my house? It's improper of you to visit at my private home. Call Monday and set up an appointment. Goodnight."

She turned and walked quickly towards her front door, but he caught up with her.

"Mrs. Ainslee since we visited your shop, I have been investigating your business and I think we should have a conversation about your setup at Crawley. Something I'm sure you would rather do here than at your shop."

Mrs. Ainslee quickened her step, she was only a couple of feet from her front door and although the officer's voice was calm and appeared sympathetic, she felt intimidated by his size and his closeness. His mention of the word Crawley startled her, and she hurried even more to reach the safety of her home.   Just as she turned her key in the lock his voice whispered over her shoulder.

"Let's go in and talk, shall we? Much more comfortable inside." and he pushed open her front door pushing her ahead into the house.

"How dare you? If you don't leave now, I'll call my husband down instantly."

"Forget it Mrs. Ainslee, or should I call you Smith? Betty Smith formerly married to Freddy Smith who now resides in Her Majesty's Prison, Pentonville. And before you say anything, I also know that both your children are currently abroad."

Blount walked across the hallway to her lounge and made himself comfortable. He waited patiently for her to follow.

"You know that's what first interested me in your case. I wondered how a woman, whose former husband was only a second storey man, could afford to send her daughter to the best finishing school in Paris and give her son enough money to set up a gambling casino in Monaco. With rationing still on we know there's not a lot of money in frocks, yet you have opened several other shops and seem to have money to spare. I asked myself how Betty Smith can do this while other shopkeepers struggle. Just where did the money come from me asked myself?"

"None of your damn business?" snarled Mrs. Ainslee.

"Oh, but it is my business, I am a policeman, remember?   I want to know all about your business arrangements. How it is that you produce top of the line labels, yet your firm doesn't deal directly with any of those fashion houses?"

"Get lost. I'm not telling you a bloody thing," she shouted at him.

"Well then I'll tell you how I think it happens and then when I take you in, we can confirm it with your people in Crawley." Blount went on "I think that either you sneak in a camera to the shows or that you employ somebody who can sketch details of the gowns as they come on display. These are then sent to your Crawley factory, along with similar but cheaper material samples. It's there that the designs are made up and fraudulently labelled and then sent to you for distribution to your shops or to others willing to pay your prices. During my investigation I found that the factory in Crawley is not in your name but is a shell company. How am I doing so far?"

She sat silently in her armchair looking down at her feet as she considered her situation. Finally.

"I know your sort I've come across rotten coppers before. So how much do you want?"

"Three hundred pounds a month. To be passed over at a place of my choosing. The money must be from a general account and you must not draw the money out separately. I don't want your accountant asking awkward questions."

And so, it began. Four and a half years of being constantly afraid of losing her business. She had been prepared to continue the payments but a few months ago, Blount had made a tactical error by making contact with her daughter and then she knew that her arrangement with him had to come to an end. Determined not to lose her business she began to make arrangements for a visit to Mr. Smith of Pentonville. Her ex would know just the person needed for this kind of work. But it would take time to arrange.

WPC Jenkins had prepared a listing of all the records found in Blount's files which now included the amounts of money and the dates the money was collected.

"Now we have an approximate date of some of these incidents so all we have to do is to backtrack to see what notable event happened on or around those dates," said Jones as he looked up from his notes, "I see several lines of investigation; we go to our own case records to see what matches, then we examine back copies of the local paper. Thirdly we have to interview all officers and civilian workers who had any connection whatsoever with Blount, to see what they can remember. We should make contact with his former superiors in Newcastle. What do you think Smith?"

"I think that could yield some good information but," the older man hesitated.

"But what Sgt?" asked Jones.

"I would like to go back out to Steyning to poke around at the murder site and also find out more about that young man, Stuart Hughes, and see why he was at the Baxter house in the spring, "explained Smith. "I feel the house at Steyning has a bigger connection to this murder than perhaps we think it has."

"Good man. Have you a summary of the interviews from the Baxter House and the neighbours? We should go and speak again to some of the locals especially the shopkeepers, they usually know more than anybody about the local goings on. Also let the solicitor Mr. Siddely know that we will be stopping by later this afternoon with some more questions regarding the tenants and the original owner."

It was a beautiful bright day as Smith drove along the coast to Shoreham. Just as he turned to follow the river road to Steyning raindrops began to hit the windshield.

"Does it always rain in Steyning?" asked Jones.

"Seems like it. Look Sir we are just passing the place where they found young Bobby's car."

Both men looked out across to the old brick works.

"I wonder how his folks are managing, do you hear from the Williams' at all?" asked Smith.

"Yes. I arranged for the beat man to pop in now and again and he lets me know how things are. Mrs. Williams goes up to the cemetery every day after walking the girls to school. Mr. Williams seems okay although not as friendly as he used to be according to neighbours."

"Well it will take years for them to get over Bobby's death. I don't know how I would manage if it were our boy who was killed," replied Smith. Both men sat quietly, immersed in their own memories of the brutal murder of young Bobby Williams.

CHAPTER TEN

She had finished the washing and with her husband now at Westminster and her sons at university she was, as usual, alone. Constantly being left alone was not the life she had envisioned when her husband, decorated many times for his daring exploits as a bomber pilot, returned from the War. She remembered the excitement at his homecoming. At last, she had thought, the boys would have their father back and I would have my husband. She especially looked forward to the resumption of their rather quiet country life, she as a housewife and mother and he as the local solicitor and member of the Parish Council. She remembered how she looked forward to many years of quiet happiness as she and her husband would watch their sons grow into men.

After the initial happiness and readjustment of being a complete family small cracks began to show in their relationship. Her husband returned to his family certainly a war hero but also a very changed man. Always inclined to be quiet and reserved he was now given to periods of melancholy which suddenly switched to impatient actions, such as crushing the newspaper rather than his usual habit of folding it neatly. She had also noticed a change in his voice, it was much sharper, more strident and in conversation had an impatient ring about it.

The root of his problems came to light one evening early in the New Year. It was after dinner and they were both reading when suddenly he stood up strode across to the mantelpiece, lit his pipe and in a very calm voice announced that he was bored with their village life and wanted to do something more active and certainly more meaningful with his life. It caught her by surprise and her first thought was that he was abandoning her, especially as of late he grown less and less attentive to her needs and physical desires. But his next statement left no doubt as to his ambitions.

"The incumbent M.P. old Rogers, is well past his prime, so I'm going to oppose him in the coming election."

She was shocked. Nothing had been said before. He hadn't consulted her nor sought her support. He had just made up his mind on his own.

"What about us?" she remembered calling out. " What about the boys and their futures?"

"Oh, I have thought all about that. In fact, their future is what this is all about. When I am successful the boys will have many more career doors open to them. They will have opportunities to mix with the right kind of men. Men who already have some sway in this country, who can help the boys get on in life. They will meet the daughters of affluent parents and possibly marry into the aristocracy. People they would never meet if they were stuck here in this quiet little backwater forever."

He stopped to draw on his pipe. She stood up

"What about me then what will I do?" her voice breaking with fear for her own future.

"Oh my dear, you silly thing you will still be my wife. You will keep this house going while I live in London and you will have lots of time for your gardening and your afternoon teas with friends. You do realize that it is imperative that while I'm in London you must be seen as the good supportive wife here in my constituency. We must keep the local voters happy at all times. Everything will be fine dear, just go on as usual." He went to walk away but she put out her hand to stop him.

"When will we tell the boys?" she asked.

"Oh, they have known for several weeks now. We have already formed a campaign committee with some affluent locals, and we intend to begin in earnest next month."

She was left just staring into space as he left the room. What had just happened to her nice, quiet ordered world? Then the anger came, she rose quickly following him into his office.

"Why wasn't I consulted? I am part of this family you have no right to exclude me in decisions as important as this?" She took a deep breath, "Do you not love me anymore?" her voice faltered more than she had wished.

"Oh, my dear this has nothing to do with love. You are my wife. We have just fought a terrible war and now we must get this country back on its feet. We must have a government that is able to make hard decisions. We must elect men who are not afraid to be unpopular to get the right things done. Love has no place in the government of the next generation. You are a sensible woman you must understand how things are now."

He turned away from her back to his papers, he saw no need to comfort her. To him the matter was closed. It was then she knew her life would never be the same.

His campaign started slowly with meetings held at the house where she could be part of the team but as it gained momentum and the team increased in number a decision was made to rent the nearby empty hall. Gradually their entire family life became subservient to the Campaign. Nobody had warned her of the amount of work involved in running a political campaign, nor did she expect the continual intrusion into her family life or the unexpected passion of the young people who gathered around her husband. As the campaign picked up speed, she felt herself gradually being shut out. At times she was allowed to accompany her husband as he canvassed the various neighbourhoods but as for input, all the ideas, strategies and collected information was looked after by the bright young people on the team.

She grew irritated at being viewed by campaign workers as being the supportive wife, the caring mother who looked after the family needs and most of all she hated being referred to as the 'tea lady of the campaign'. She was even more irritated by the almost hero worship of her husband, 'the answer to all our prayers' was expressed several times, especially by the more opinionated young women. After a few weeks she gave up trying to fit in and stayed at home rather than trooping off to be ignored at Campaign Headquarters.

The few times when her husband insisted that she attend some function or other there were always smart young men ready to give her a lift back to her house. On one particular occasion the young driver seemed to be making a concerted effort to make her feel part of what was going on. He spoke to her respectfully, asked her how she was coping with all the hustle and bustle and when entering the house even offered to make her a cup of tea. She was quite flattered by his attentions and each time she needed a ride the same young man would be eager to drive her home.

It was late one evening, when her husband was staying overnight in London on a Party matter that she made her fateful mistake. She allowed the friendly bantering to go too far until the comments became sexual innuendos which led to her being far too friendly and suggestive. She was swept away by this young man's attention and in a daze of desire she seduced him into her bed. Their passionate affair lasted for a fortnight, that is when the reality of what she was risking suddenly hit her and she put an end to it.

The election was just two days away, her husband was out canvassing, and she was returning from having dinner with a friend when she noticed a strange car in her drive. Probably one of the campaign people she thought as she unlocked the front door.

"Mrs. Stewart?"

"Yes. I expect you are looking for my husband. He is out canvassing they'll tell you where he is at the Hall. Just go on down the road and it's by the Green." She swung around to shut the door thinking the visitor had gone. Instead he was very close behind her actually preventing her from closing the door.

"Who are you, what do you want?"

"I'm Sgt. Blount with the Sussex Constabulary and I need to speak with you Mrs. Stewart."

"Well what is it? Come in but I am very busy."

"Mrs. Stewart we are here to investigate a complaint from a woman that you, Mrs. Stewart, seduced her young son and are continuing to have an affair with him."

"What, this is ridiculous. Who on earth is this woman and who is her young son?"

"A Mrs. Bellman and her son's name is Joshua Bellman."

"But Josh is over twenty years old, what is she on about?"

"Do you deny having an affair with this young man?" he produced a photo.

"I did have a relationship but it's all over now. But he said he was almost twenty-one."

"Here is his birth certificate, see he is just eighteen. Big for his age wasn't he Mrs. Stewart?" She fled to the bathroom and vomited when the realization of what this could mean to her family hit her. Rinsing her face, she went back downstairs to find that the policemen were still there.

"I suppose you are going to charge me now?" she asked

"That is what should happen. Is there any reason why not?" She looked back at the Sgt. Blount turned to his companion.

"Constable wait outside by the car for me."

"What are you hinting at?" she asked when the young constable had left.

"Well a charge like this would be very stressful on your marriage and most certainly put paid to your husband's political hopes."

She paced about her room. Arms crossed over her chest. Hands tightly clenched. She felt sick again with fear of what might be and anger at her own stupidity which now placed her family's future in this man's hand. She turned abruptly.

"Well what do you want of me?"

"I can take care of the boy's mother, but you will have to pay me to get the charge dropped."

Blount moved forward until he physically towered over her.

"This is what you will do," And then proceeded to go through his routine regarding monthly payments.

Her secret had been kept and paid for almost four years but now that her husband was rumoured to be in the running for a Cabinet post she knew that somehow, she must put a stop to Blount. Unable to own up to her indiscretions she decided that somehow, she had to get rid of Blount.

When Jones and Smith reached Steyning they parked the car at the top end of the winding main street and started to walk back down the narrow pavement. The house to house had been a residential survey but Smith felt that businesspeople were much more attentive to local gossip or information.

Jones had driven through Steyning many times before, but he was always on the way to somewhere else. One of his greatest enjoyments was to walk for miles over the hills and dales of Sussex. By now he knew and had travelled most of the public pathways that crisscrossed the South Downs and had become familiar with many of the small communities that lay nestled against the its curves. Away from the wind and gales that drove down the Channel and more importantly had provided a shelter as enemy bombers headed towards London. For the citizens of these tightly knit communities the war appeared to be more an inconvenience than the everyday danger it was to the citizens living on the south side of the Downs.

To Dai Jones the main street of the village looked like a scene out of Dickens with its cobbled streets, very narrow pavements and overhanging windows with their small leaded panes of glass. Jones was a good walker, but he soon grew impatient with having to hop up and down off the pavement, dodging elbows and shopping baskets and the continual buzz of conversation. After a while he waved across to Smith indicating they meet. They stood in the forecourt of the Post Office to exchange notes.

"Pretty village," said Jones, "but they need wider pavements."

"Always a problem in these small places. But wait 'til the double-deckers start running then the locals will have to keep their eyes open."

"When are they due?"

"Quite soon so I heard." Smith chuckled. "Just thinking of them going down this road makes me wonder how many accidents will happen. At present the pedestrians own the road here but that will come to an end with the buses."

"Did you find anything new for us along your side?"

"No bank accounts for Blount. Old Mr. Pope had been a widower for only a short time. Nobody knew anything about the Fletchers other than they came from up north and then left for Australia. Oh, I did find from the grocer that old Mr. Pope had his groceries delivered to the house every week. What about you any luck?"

"Nothing so far but there's both a butchers and a greengrocers further down on my side."

"Let's try there and ask specifically about deliveries to Baxter House."

While Smith went in the butcher's Jones went to the greengrocers. Both shops had queues of housewives but eventually Smith and Jones were able to ask their questions. It seemed that Jones was destined not to get any new information.

"No officer I don't know anything about the people up at Baxter's. My boy would ride up on his bike and drop off the order at the back door. The money for last week's order would be on the windowsill and he would bring it straight back to me, here at the shop. Can't help you I'm afraid," explained the man turning away to serve the next customer.

But Smith was luckier for the shop was almost empty by the time it was his turn, so the butcher was willing to chat.

"Apparently." Smith related to Jones."When Mrs. Pope died Mr. Pope used to order his meat a week in advance and it was always the same things, chops, stewing beef, leg of lamb and sausages."

"Did he come down to get it?"

"For a while he did but then he wanted it delivered so the butcher's wife used to deliver it in their van. The wife never saw Mr. Pope as the housekeeper always answered the door and together, they would take the order into the kitchen."

"Did you find out the housekeeper's name?'

"Apparently they only knew her as Bertha. The butcher saw her once or twice around the shops but really didn't know her. He was saying that she might have gone into Shoreham to do other shopping."

"At least we know now that there is another person who was familiar with Baxter House," agreed Jones. "Bertha isn't much to go on but perhaps Mr. Siddely knows more about her. Let's hope so. Now I want to stop by at the Trent's office and then we'll see Siddely on the way home."

Their visit to the estate agents did not take long. In fact, Smith stayed in the car writing up his notes as Jones said he would only be a few minutes. Sure enough within minutes Jones was back in the car urging Smith to get started for the trip to Hove. Smith looked sideways at his boss, but Jones was sitting looking out of the window seemingly smiling at the rain. Jones had never married, much to his mother's despair. Had never had a girlfriend to Smith's knowledge. But the sergeant had a suspicion that young Miss Willcott just might change his Inspector's thoughts about that.

Mr. Siddely was a man of the old school. He wore a pinstriped suit, a silver waistcoat, white shirt and silver tie. His round face gave him an almost cherubic appearance spoilt only by a pair of flint ice blue eyes that seemed to see everything that a client was trying to hide. Jones liked him straight away.

"Come in gentleman," the older man said offering a handshake to both officers. "I know you are here about the Baxter House and the body that was found there but how can I help you?"

"We need details about the previous owners and or tenants and also anyone else who you know had access to the house."

The solicitor opened the file.

"Mr. Pope owned the house; he inherited it from his father. It was originally bought by the grandfather sometime in the late 1800s. When the younger Mr. Pope died it was passed to a Mrs. James, his niece who had gone to Canada to live. She didn't want it, so we let it to a Mr. and Mrs. Fletcher who lived there with their adopted son Stuart. Then they immigrated to Australia. Now it is up for sale. Probably you know all this. It is not a complicated matter, at least it wasn't until you found the body there." Mr. Siddely sat back in his chair.   "I heard that the victim was one of yours, is that true?"

"Yes Mr. Siddely the victim is or at least was a member of the Sussex Constabulary until he left."

Mr. Siddely was embarrassed and fidgeted in his chair.

"That will be hard for the Force. Any clues yet as to why?"

"All I can tell you is that we are continuing with our enquiries round and about the Steyning area trying to put together a history of the house and the people who lived there. We were hoping that you could help us regarding any casual workers that would have had knowledge of the inside of the house."

"Mrs. Pope always hired a window cleaner, a Fred Warner, unfortunately he was killed out in Germany in the last month of the war. Let's see who else was there?"

Mr. Siddely swung his chair around towards the large window that looked directly out to the Channel and sat for a moment tapping the tips of his forefingers together. Suddenly turning back to his desk, he announced.

"There was an odd job man, but he died too. Oh, but when his wife died, Mr. Pope's wife that is, he hired a woman to come in to clean for him and do the odd cooking etc. Now what was her name?"

The solicitor went back to his window gazing then suddenly turned back again.

"Her name was Bertha Rowington I should have remembered because Mr. Pope left her a small cottage over Ditchling way. As Mr. Pope's executor I saw to the business myself. The large house, as we said, went to his niece Mrs. James."

"Do you know if this Miss Rowington is still in the cottage now?"

"I haven't heard that she has moved. Everything was provided for in his will, so she had nothing legal left to worry about. Probably only what she would do with the cottage when she dies, as I believe she is a single lady. So, I haven't had contact with her since she moved in."

CHAPTER ELEVEN

The Saturday night performance had been spectacular. The entire cast was jubilant with their success. It had been a good week one where everything seemed to go well. Nobody fluffed their lines; the props were all laid out in their correct order to be picked up when needed. The audience was most receptive, and the critics had been kind, even the couple of London reviewers were generous with their praise.

The director announced that it was party time around at the pub and the noisy, excited cast gradually moved to the stage door and out onto New Road to the corner pub. Martin Davies was as excited and giddy as the others. This was the first time that he had played the leading male role. As a tall, dark haired, muscular man he fitted the requirements of the romantic role perfectly.

"The hero who always got his girl," was one quote from the local paper.

Davies was thrilled as the cast gathered around him at the pub and thanking him for his performance while toasting everyone's continued success. His response was equally kind to the others and then took the cast back to the bar for another round. Some of the younger cast hung around Martin, gushingly admiring all the time hoping that they would be the one he walked home that evening. Davies was not married, nor in any known relationship so he was fair game for the opposite sex, young or even those of more mature years. But by two o'clock in the morning he had had enough.

"I'm off home," he announced to everyone "Goodnight, see you tomorrow afternoon, no" he corrected himself, "see you this afternoon, for rehearsal."

But Martin Davies did not go home to his Royal Crescent flat instead he worked his way down through the backstreets, across North St into East St. For him the real celebration had not even begun. He needed and wanted more, and he knew just the right club where he would find his friend who was always a willing partner to Martin's wishes. For Martin Davies, despite his outward appearance and apparent style of living, was a homosexual.

It was a week later just as Davies was dressing ready to go to the theatre when there was a loud knock on his flat door.

"Just a minute," he called out," almost ready. "But it wasn't his expected guest it was a large bearded policeman.

"Mr. Davies?"

"Yes. What do you want? I have to leave for the theatre."

"Ah yes, the theatre. May I come in Sir, just for a moment?"

"Very well but I am in a tearing hurry."

"Just take a minute Sir. You see we have had a complaint laid against you."

"What. By whom?"

"A young lad, not even twenty."

Davies heart stopped cold, there was a thundering in his ears and he was unable to focus on the individual in front of him. He managed to walk away from the door to a chair. The bearded man followed and closed the door behind him.

"What did he say?"

"Oh, so you know the young man then?"

"No. I just want to know what the complaint is."

"Importuning."

Davies felt for the arm of chair as he sat down. While the policeman went on about the young man's statement at the station all Davies felt was fear.

"It seems that you and the young man in question had an altercation outside the Club 54, on Saturday the 24th. Do you remember that fight Sir?"

"Yes."

"How did it start?"

"I can't remember. It was very late, and I had been celebrating, and I was waiting for Jonathan."

"Did you friend arrive?"

"Yes, but he was with somebody else, so I started talking to this other fellow."

"According to witnesses you said something to him and next thing you were both outside on the pavement fighting."

"Well since when has a barroom brawl been a crime?"

"It seems that you asked the younger man to go upstairs to a private room and have sex with you. That is the crime."

Davies was distraught. Although he knew other actors who importuned young boys but to be actually publicly accused of this is a court of law would most definitely put an end to his theatre career. Just as he had tasted success too. The officer was still talking at him, but Davies wasn't listening to the man's voice droning on. He could only think of his career and the disgrace this would bring. How his dear parents would die of shame when they read about this in the newspaper.

Slowly Davies realized that the droning voice had changed. Instead of being accusatory the officer seemed to be more understanding and seemed to be offering Davies a way out of his predicament. Through the haze of words Davies picked out the word 'proposal 'and then 'agreement 'but then the voice hardened as Sgt. Blount struck home with his blackmail plan.

It didn't take Davies long to agree to everything that Blount proposed as long as the charges would be dropped.

In his London flat near Victoria Station, Davies thought of all the money he had handed over to Blount each month for almost four years. He remembered the meetings, usually in some country lane and he thought of the sheer evil of the man. Davies had become very successful and respected in the theatre world and as his fame grew, he worried constantly that Blount would betray him, so he concocted a plan to finally rid himself of. Today he would make the fateful phone call,

"And soon my evil torturer you will be gone, and I will still be here." With that he twirled his scarf around his neck and left his flat murmuring "Now that my little plan is planned, so to speak, I will give the best performance of my life tonight." as he bounded down the stairs two steps at a time.

Returning to his office Jones found three memos on his desk blotter. The first from the mechanic who had taken Blount's cars for inspection; he needed to speak to either Jones or Smith urgently first thing in the morning. The second note was from Masters saying he had information from his visit to the pubs earlier that day. The last memo was from Supt. Young who wanted to see Jones as soon as he returned from Steyning. Just as Jones was leaving to see the Supt. Smith knocked and entered Jones's office.

"It seems that Atkinson was able to match up three of those coded tabs with incidents from the local paper. He is waiting now with the details; can you see him?"

"No not just now, the Super wants to see me. I don't know how long I will be, but you and Atkinson start, and I'll be along as soon as I can."

Jones really hoped that this meeting was just an update for the Super. He was very conscious how difficult this investigation was not only for Blount's former colleagues but also for the senior officers as the integrity of the Sussex Constabulary was at stake. Although Jones was not a member of the force during Blount's time and was a little more detached from the internal concerns, he still felt a keen loyalty to the Force and the community that he had accepted as his own, to serve and protect.

"Come in Dai as you can imagine this investigation has been most unsettling for the men. Many of them knew Blount personally and although most did not like him the manner of his death is worrying."

"Yes sir, I can see that, but my instinct is that it was an outside killing. I 'm sure that his murder is tied up with the records that we found in his storage unit. Once we untangle those and find his bank accounts, we will have a much better idea of motive. I believe that Blount was blackmailing citizens that he had come into contact with during his policing duties, we just need to identify them."

"Of course, you have whatever resources you need to get this over quickly and I'll do my best to keep the Chief Constable out of your way," added the Supt.

"Thank you, sir, that would be a real help. There is one other thing you could do and that is to make contact with your counterpart in Newcastle and see what else you can find out about Blount and what he was into up there. See if you can find out who he worked with and if they knew anything about his outside activities when he was stationed there."

"Do you think that someone from up north did it?"

"We have to try all lines of investigation not only up north but also all the officers down here that worked with him. The most puzzling issue is trying to make a connection between Blount and the house in Steyning."

"I will make sure that you get the records of all our men who served during Blount's time. Some will be retired but I'll make the call and get them in. When do you want to start that?"

"As soon as I have the names, I'll get Jenkins to set up an appointment list. Hopefully by the end of the week."

"Good and I'll get on to Newcastle this afternoon."

Smith was still in his office when Jones returned.

"Okay then let's hear what Atkinson has found."

"Three events that match the dates and the initials. There was a break in at a shop in Lancing. The shop was owned by a Mrs. Irene Ainslee. According to the newspaper the shop was trashed. The owner was away, and her assistant Ellen Strong called it in. The date and initials match the tab on this folder. Next one is a scuffle that was reported outside the Club 54 on East Street. That is the only incident reported that day. We don't have names, but the date is right and perhaps the club owner will know who the men were. The third incident is of a hit and run accident out near Ditchling, a young boy died of his injuries. The car was later found and its owner, a Mr. Palmer, told the police that the car had been stolen. Both the dates and the owner's name match the tab on this folder."

"So, we have two definites and one maybe, a good start. Now finally we can find out what Blount was up to."

"How did you get on with the Super?"

"I asked him to contact Newcastle and he promised whatever resources we needed. Also, he will get the men together for interviews. He is very uncomfortable with what is going on, he's taking it personally and it seems that our old friend the C.C. is not being the most helpful. But now, thanks to Atkinson we have quite a list of people to interview. I suggest we go over to Ditchling to see Mr. Palmer about the car incident and then we can visit Mr. Pope's former housekeeper who also lives in Ditchling. Did you get her address from the solicitor?"

"Yes. Give me five minutes to check on Jenkins and Atkinson and I'll be ready."

When they were on their way out Jones remembered the memo from the mechanic that he had passed on to Smith.

"Did you get to the garage?"

"Sorry. Yes, that was good. The mechanic found a secret compartment under the back of the driver's seat, wrapped in brown paper, were two bank books from Barclays of Littlehampton, so I am sending Masters along to check them out. I did call the bank manager."

Jones felt very satisfied with the morning's work, at last they were making some progress. They had people to interview and he was confident that soon the connection between the murder and Baxter house would reveal itself. He sat back in the car relaxed, enjoying the drive through the Sussex countryside.

CHAPTER TWELVE

According to the map the house should be just around the corner. It's called The Grange." But it wasn't a house they arrived at but a pair of tall black iron gates.

"Are we at the right place?" asked Jones.

"Yes, but by the look of the grounds this is obviously a private school not a residential house." Just then an older man in a uniform stepped out of the sentry-box style hut and asked what they wanted. When they asked for Mr. Palmer he explained.

"Mrs. Palmer lives in that house at the edge of the fields. But she is still in mourning and will not see anybody. Her husband, the late headmaster, died a few weeks ago. Very tragic, and now she has to move out of the house to make room for the new headmaster."

Anxious to keep the flow of information going Smith asked.

"What made his death so tragic?"

"Well it was like this, although you didn't hear nothing from me, but Mr. Palmer liked his drink. Oh, he was a good headmaster. He had been here about twenty years but a few years back he started drinking more heavily and earlier in the day. The students noticed and began to make fun of him, so the Governors put him on notice to stop drinking or lose his position. Oh, he did stop for a while but then something started him up again and that was it according to my information. He threw himself in the duck pond over there." he said pointing to the side of the main building. "He was found by the gardener."

"Thanks for your help Mr....?"

"Bert Greenslade actually but just call me Bert,"

"Please let us through as we have to speak to Mrs. Palmer on another official matter."

"I will and I wish you luck, you'll know what I mean when you meet her."

"I wonder what he meant by that," commented Jones as Smith drove the car through the gates and onto the grounds of the Grange.

To the left of the drive were two football pitches while on the right they saw two pairs of rugby goalposts. The main building was three stories high and constructed in the traditional red brick of Sussex although much of the outside was covered in green ivy. The main building seemed to consist of three parts; a centre section that had large double doors where the drive circled around. To each side were sections that had several entrances, although much less impressive than the main one. Further off were more recently constructed buildings that looked to be more utilitarian, perhaps classrooms. The house that the officers wanted was at the end of a lane away from the main drive. It was a two-storey building and identical in style to the main building. Surrounded by well cared for shrubbery it gave the perception of being part of yet separate from the rest of the grounds.

Smith knocked respectfully on the front door, then with no response tried again with a sharper more urgent rap. Just as the officers were considering going around to the back the door opened very slightly. A timid voice reached the men.

"Mrs. Palmer isn't receiving any visitors. She said to take whatever you are selling and leave her property."

"Please tell Mrs. Palmer that we are officers from the Sussex Constabulary, and we wish to speak with her."

The door closed again, and the men were left on the doorstep. A slight movement at the door,

"Mrs. Palmer says that she has had enough of policemen and if you don't leave, she will telephone her friend the Chief Constable and complain about your aggressive behaviour."

"That's it. Friends or not with the C.C. we are going in!" and with that Jones eased the door open and strode past the hapless maid.

"What is the meaning of this? You cannot just walk into my house without my permission?" stated the loud and authoritative voice from the sitting room.

"Yes, ma'am I can, my warrant card gives me that permission. We are here simply to get some answers about an incident that took place several years ago. Our visit would be over much quicker if you would be cooperative and answer our questions."

Mrs. Palmer was a well-built lady of around her middle fifties. She was dressed in traditional county clothes, sensible shoes, a tweed skirt and a salmon coloured twinset. Her outfit was completed by triple string of what Jones could see were real pearls. Her curly auburn hair was severely pinned back, and her face showed little traces of makeup but that is where the nice part came to an end for she wore an expression so haughty, so distasteful, that she was difficult to look at.

"I simply will not answer any of your questions. This is preposterous I will not speak to you anymore."

"Well Madam you have two choices we can stay here, and you can answer our questions, or we will set up a meeting at the Brighton Police Station when we will do the questioning. I will add madam that these questions are not about your late husband's death but about a stolen car several years ago. We came out here to speak to your husband not knowing that he had died."

She continued to stride to and fro across the room fidgeting with her lace handkerchief.

"Did you know that the Board of Governors is making me leave this house at the end of term? After everything that William did for them to improve the school just because he's dead they are throwing me out without anywhere to go. No insurance because he killed himself and nowhere to live, what am I to do?" She spoke with an imperious voice that demanded attention.

"Do you have family?" asked Smith softly.

"No, I do not. William always thought that the students were enough children in his life, but I always wanted my own children," she lifted her head and her eyes were dark with anger.

"Whenever I mentioned it, he always changed the subject and because of him I am now alone."

Jones and Smith waited patiently as she came to a halt.

Turning to Jones she said, "For heaven's sake sit down and tell me what you want to know and then I can be rid of you."

"Mrs. Palmer do you remember a few years ago, five years actually, when your husband had his car stolen?"

"Yes, I do. I'm not likely to forget that incident. One of your men came here to our house and accused my husband of killing a child. He said that William had run the boy down as the boy was walking down a country road. Not far from here actually."

"Do you remember the officer's name?"

"What does that matter? William explained that he was on his way to the local Station to report that his car had been stolen the evening before. According to your man William's car had been found in a ditch nearby the accident. It was badly damaged from the crash or from contact with the boy. It was never determined." She became indignant once more.

"But why is this being dragged up again. William was cleared and the case closed."

"Yes, we understand that Mrs. Palmer," Jones explained patiently. "But if you could remember the officer's name that would be really helpful."

"There were two policemen; the sergeant was in charge, but the younger officer was taking a lot of notes."

Jones and Smith looked at each other realizing that the idea of there being another officer involved had not occurred to either man. Jones tried again.

"Please try and remember all that you can from that meeting Mrs. Palmer."

"He was a big man that sergeant. He spoke roughly to William, very uncouth kind of man." She sniffed," probably a bully to the younger men. I seemed to recall his name started with B."

Smith asked if he had ever returned to the house

"No but William had to go into Brighton to see him and sign some papers about it. I remember William telling me about that."

Jones stood up

"Mrs. Palmer I am going to ask you two questions that perhaps seem out of line but are very important to our enquires."

"Go ahead ask your dreadful questions, get on with it," she said as her hands continued to flutter in her lap.

"When did your husband's drinking habits become noticeable?"

Mrs. Palmer was out of her chair and striding across to Jones her face a mask of fury.

"What are you implying Inspector that my husband was a drunk. How dare you."

Smith stood up to cut off the angry woman in mid-flight.

"I know this is painful and we are sorry to have to ask these questions, but we believe his drinking increased after the incident with the stolen car," continued Jones.

By now Mrs. Palmer was a broken woman sobbing into her handkerchief.

"He did his drinking away from me and the school. Always took off somewhere to be alone. This started about a year after the car was stolen. Often, I asked him what the matter was, but he would not tell me. You'll probably find out that the Board of Governors were going to dismiss him from his position because of the drinking. I didn't know about that until I read the letter, he wrote the night before he died. He wrote that he was sorry for the trouble he had caused the school and me." She thumped her hand on the arm of her chair. "Even then I was only an afterthought."

The room was silent as both men waited for the distraught lady to gather herself.

"You said you had two questions?"

"Yes. This one concerns money, your money actually."

She looked up in surprise, "Why are you asking about my personal affairs. It has nothing to do with that car incident."

"We believe it has. Mrs. Palmer we are investigating the murder of a former policeman who we think was the sergeant who came to your house regarding the car."

"Is that the body found in Baxter House over in Steyning. I had heard about that. Surely you don`t think that my William had anything to do with that business?"

"No but we now know that Sgt. Blount was blackmailing citizens that he had come across in his policing duties. That is why I would like to know if you noticed any changes in your money situation."

"I didn't know anything about our finances until our bank manger called me in after William's death. Mr. Tait was concerned and had been for several years about the gradual climbing of our expenses. I explained that William had never spoken to me about money matters. But according to Mr. Tait there are several thousand pounds less in my account than should have been. I don't know what William did with his money. I have none of my own, just a small inheritance from my father but as that went into a joint account even that is almost gone now."

Jones rose to leave knowing that Mr. and even Mrs. Palmer had been victims of Blount's blackmail schemes.

"Thank you for your help Mrs. Palmer. We have what we needed and I'm sure we will not be bothering you again."

The two officers left the house each assessing how Mrs. Palmer's information would move along their investigation. Bert was waiting at the gates. Smith called out their thanks as they left, and Bert saluted them.

"Now we know what he meant. Mrs. Palmer certainly is a force to be reckoned with, but she is also a lady who will find the future a struggle without her husband's prestigious position and his salary."

"Do you think Palmer could have killed Blount?"

"No. I think we'll find that he was dead before Blount was murdered. I think we have a case of a drunken headmaster who ran down and killed that boy and then ran into Blount and his blackmailing scheme. He made an excellent victim for the Sgt."

"I was surprised," said Smith "at the mention of another man with Blount. Nobody at the station has mentioned working with the Sgt. Of course, we have had several younger officers who went into the military and some who transferred out to other stations to fill vacancies. I should have thought of that."

"When the Supt. gets his list together, we can sort that out. Meanwhile it's on to see the late Mr. Pope's housekeeper."

The former housekeeper lived in a small cottage just outside Ditchling village. A typical country cottage, with white plastered walls and tiny odd shaped windows, a fenced front garden that was a mass of flowers and shrubs and a front pathway almost hidden under the trailing flowers. The door was white with a heavy black letter box and an equally heavy old-fashioned knocker. Smith tapped on the door, which was quickly opened, although not too far, by a short, frail, elderly woman.

"Yes, what do you want?"

Her voice was thin and reedy and matched her bird like figure. She peered through thick lenses at the officers standing there. Smith explained who they were and showed their warrant cards. She opened the door and stepped forward to peer at each of the men. It was obvious that they had interrupted her baking as both her apron and her tiny hands were covered in flour, but she invited them in.

"Do sit down. I am Bertha Rowington are you sure it's me you want to see?" she squeaked.

"You are the former housekeeper for the late Mr. Pope?"

She agreed and went on to explain that she had worked at Baxter house for about ten years. She had been employed by Mrs. Pope but when her employer died, the housekeeper stayed on to do for Mr. Pope. Certainly, she knew about the passage from the summerhouse to the cellar. No, she didn't have a car and she had been back to Baxter House just once since old Mr. Pope had passed on. She didn't know anything about the Fletcher's or their son, but when she passed by on the bus, she had noticed that the house was up for sale. Apart from being widowed and having no children there was little more she could tell them.

"Not much to learn from there," remarked Smith as they drove away. "I can't really see a frail old lady like her killing Blount and then cutting him up and wheeling him through that tunnel, can you sir?"

"No, and she doesn't appear to have any connection with Blount at all. She has a nice little cottage and some money from old Mr. Pope how could there be any connection other than the Baxter house?" Jones murmured to himself and finally spoke up.

"Now that we have to go through Steyning I want to call in at Trent's to see if they have found out anymore."

"Any more about what sir?" Although Smith knew exactly what his younger companion meant."

While waiting in the car Smith reminisced about his courtship of Helen. He had been a probationary constable and they met at a New Year's dance. He and a few of his mates had gone up to London and it was there at the Palais just off Victoria Street, that he met Helen. She was bright, bubbly and she loved to dance. She always said that she loved the feel of her dress as it swished about to the rhythm of the music. She was going to a Secretary school in London but eventually wanted a job outside of the dirty city.

They corresponded by letter and just as Helen was finishing up her course a position of secretary become vacant at the Station. Smith remembered Helen's nervousness as she waited outside the Supt's office for her interview. He smiled to himself remembering how he'd hovered around, discreetly passing by her several times as she waited to be called in. He remembered her smart grey suit and black high heels and thinking that she just had to get that job. Now here it is was twenty years later, still happy together and being blessed with two boys. Smith stirred in his seat muttering out loud.

"Sometimes mixed blessings, now that they are teenagers."
But he smiled knowing that they were just typical kids struggling to find their way in this world that must seem upside down, at times to children.

Jones came flying down the three steps of the Estate office and quickly climbed into the car as Smith turned over the engine.

"Well?"

"Well what?"

"Did you get any more information from Mr. Trent?"

"Err no I didn't."

"Did you see Miss Wilcott?"

"Yes, we chatted."

"Ah," was all Smith said as he drove the car down the river road, out of Steyning towards Shoreham and then to the office at Brighton.

CHAPTER THIRTEEN

Jones had the day all planned. He would see what Masters found in Littlehampton. Then hopefully the Supt. had made some progress with his list and Smith could interview some of the officers who knew Blount. Then in the early afternoon he and Smith would visit Mrs. Ainslee to see what she had to say. Just as he was about to call in Masters, Jenkins knocked on his door.

"Sir I have been doing more research on those files now that we have the newspaper clippings." She laid down her notes on his desk.

"This Mrs. Ainslee has only been in business a few years and her real name is Betty Smith. She is divorced and her husband, Freddy Smith, is doing time for fraud in Pentonville. With Club 54 on East Street I called and spoke to the manager," she referred to her notes. "A Cyril Blake. He has been there for at least ten years. A surly beggar. Oh, sorry sir. But he was very rude on the telephone."

"That's all right Jenkins Sgt. Smith and I will sort him out tomorrow."

"Who are we sorting out tomorrow? "Smith asked as he walked in?"

"A certain Mr. Cyril Blake at the club on East Street. We have met him before, haven't we?"

"Indeed we have sir and I will enjoy putting his nose to the grindstone tomorrow."

"Are you ready for me sir?" It was Masters at Jones's door.

"Yes come in. Jenkins will you check out the recent death of a Mr. William Palmer, headmaster of The Grange a private boy's school out near Ditchling. Also see what else you can find out about the hit and run accident Atkinson found in the paper. Thank you."

"Now what do you have Masters?"

"I spent some time with the bank manager at Barclays in Littlehampton. He hadn't heard about the body at Steyning as he was away with the 'flu last week but when I showed him Blount's photo, he confirmed that it was his Mr. Black. The address this Mr. Black provided was a boarding house near the seafront as I found out later." The young officer took a breath, "There was over fifteen thousand pounds in his account. The money came in at regular intervals over the past five years and was always a cash deposit."

"Can the money be traced?"

"The bank manager was not very hopeful, but he did point out that some of the earlier payments had stopped while new ones were started."

"Go and work with Jenkins and see if these statements match up with the files that she is working on. Good work."

"Now, where were we? Right let's talk about the actual murder. The only connections to the Baxter House are the Fletchers, their son and the housekeeper Mrs. Rowington. Each of whom would know about the passageway. But their names have not shown up on Blount's files and according to Jenkins there are no Fs or Rs on the tabs. The Fletchers have been in Australia for a while, so they are out, and the housekeeper has not been near the place for years. Besides she is too fragile. So, we still need to find the son. Now to Blount or Ford or Black. Both his cars were in their proper places so how did he get to Steyning. Our Mr. Blount does not seem a man to ride on buses with those cars sitting there. We have confirmed that he received a good amount of money at regular intervals from various sources which to us smacks of blackmail. We know of three incidents in the newspaper that can be matched to our records. We have Mrs. Palmer's word that Blount and another officer investigated the hit and run accident. What are you thinking Jack?"

"What we need is a little bit of luck in tracking down this other officer. He could be the key to the rest of the people involved. I think we still have a long way to go on this one. Especially as there doesn't seem to be any family wanting to bury him,"

"What about his former wife?" asked Jones.

"We called her in Australia, and she said that she didn't have the money to send. She has remarried and they have just had twins so with four children to clothe and feed she just can't do it. She was very upset at the news. Of course, I didn't tell her all the gory details."

"Well that's it, we'll have to see to his burial."

Before leaving for Lancing Jones checked with Supt. Young about the list to see if he had made any contact with Newcastle. The response was that the list was almost completed but the telephone call was a disaster.

"They kept me hanging on for fifteen minutes saying they were looking for the Supt. I could hear muffled voices arguing and then after all that they said he was away sick, and would I call early next week he might be back then. Damn incompetence I call it. You know you and I should take a trip up there next week and light a fire under their behinds. They owe us for sending us an officer who they knew was rotten."

Jones' face broke into a real boyish grin.

"You know Sir I would like to be part of their awakening; shall we say. I'll make the arrangements if you like?"

He left the Supt. to his mutterings and caught up with Smith at the doorway. After recounting his conversation to Smith, the Sgt laughingly said

"Now I'm beginning to feel sorry for those idiots up north. They don't know what they are in for."

They were both laughing as they walked through the swing doors to the parking area.

Lancing was the next community past Shoreham Harbour and the small town was heralded by the famous Lancing College that sat high on the South Downs over-looking Lancing, Shoreham and the Adur River estuary. Smith explained that the building was originally built in 1848 for the sons of the aristocracy and was still privately owned and run. The College, like the traditional Public schools provided not only a first-class education but also a home for the sons of men who were world leaders. Lancing College had a worldwide reputation of providing good young men for Oxford and Cambridge.

Lancing High Street ran from the seafront north to the Old Shoreham Road and was physically cut in half by the railway station and level crossing for the frequent trains east to Brighton or west to Portsmouth and Southampton. The shop the officers was seeking was about halfway up the upper part of the High Street, at the more fashionable end.

The shop itself was quite ordinary having a centre door that separated two glass show windows. When the officers entered, they were greeted by a fresh-faced young woman who looked at them in surprise. It was not often that Ellen Strong had a man in the shop, let alone two of them. She almost bobbed as she asked if she could be of help.

"Are you Ellen Strong?"

"Yes. Who's asking?" Smith explained who they were and showed their warrant cards.

"Oh, I will call Mrs. Ainslee. You have to speak to her she is the owner."

A heavily made up woman of about forty-five pushed through the velvet curtain and almost sashayed into the main area.

"Yes. What is it?" her voice was quite soft but had that falsely, cultivated accent adopted by many who wished to hide their place of birth. Her face was hard, and her smile did not reach anywhere near her eyes. Jones explained who they were and suggested that they go into her office for further conversation. Her face hardened even more, seeming ready to resist Jones's suggestion but Ellen quickly stepped forward saying that business was slow, and she could manage the shop. Mrs. Ainslee was not happy as now she had no choice but to invite the officers through the curtain to her office.

"What do you want?" she snapped.

"We are investigating the murder of a former police officer, former Sgt. Blount who we are led to believe you knew."

"No, I have never had any dealings with an officer of that name," she answered vehemently. "What's this all about then? What has this to do with me?"

Her adopted accent began to falter as the pitch of her voice rose.

"I don't know anything. Why are you bothering me? A respectable businesswoman trying to make a living."

Jones took up her challenge. "We have evidence to prove that you became involved with Sgt. Blount when he came here when your shop was burgled."

Mrs. Ainslee opened her mouth but Jones quickly continued.

"Further we have evidence that you met with Blount, agreed to his blackmail scheme and continued to pay him monthly amounts Will you confirm that for us Mrs. Ainslee?"

"No, I will not. You have nothing on me." She stood and stared at the officers.

Jones stood up, "I would like you to come with us to the station to answer more questions. Now please Mrs. Ainslee."

"Good riddance to bad rubbish," she suddenly spat out, leaning against her small desk.

"Oh, so you did know him." Jones sat down again.

"Yes, I knew the bastard, him and his weaselly little sidekick of a constable, Waters, good name for that one, weak as water he was. When I read about Blount's murder, I opened a bottle of champagne to celebrate. He put me through years of misery with his threats and took hundreds of pounds from me."

She paced to and fro in the small office. "Oh, I prayed that someday somebody would get the sod and now he is gone. Hallelujah."

"Why were you paying him?" asked Smith.

"'Cause he found out that I was running a racket with the labels on my dresses."

"You know that you could still be prosecuted?"

"But I don't do it anymore, 'e scared me off. I'm perfectly legit now and my place in Crawley just does my summer fashions."

"Did you kill Officer Blount?"

"No. I wished he were dead many times but no I didn't kill 'im. Where would my kids be if I went to jail, with their father already…" she trailed off.

"Already what..?"

She sat down.

"Already in jail. He's just finishing up a term in Pentonville. My real name is Betty Smith, but we are divorced now. I expect you already knew that. But I didn't kill Blount. I swear. But I am very pleased that he is dead and out of my life."

"We will be in touch. Don't leave the area." With that admonition the officers left the dress shop.

"We'll put her as a definite maybe. She was honest enough about her feelings for Blount but I'm not sure that she did anything about it," remarked Jones.

"With her London background she could have found somebody to do the job for her. I would certainly keep her at the top of our list.

Unfortunately, at present she is the only likely suspect we have," muttered Smith as they both climbed into the car.

The Jaguar purred through the iron gates coming to its usual stop outside the massive front doors. Sir Michael Crandall was feeling very buoyant today. While reading his newspaper at breakfast he had seen the headlines *Former Sussex Policeman Found Dead* and was delighted to read the account of Blount's murder. "At last some brave person did what should have been done years ago."

"What did you say dear?" asked his wife.

"Oh, just complaining about the government dear." Humming away he left the table, kissed his wife and picked up his briefcase on his way out of the front door. But then he stumbled, suddenly realizing that perhaps his own plans had been carried out and he was responsible for the officer's death. Holding the door jamb for support he tried to remember exactly what had been said when he met the contractor. He, the man, was to wait for specific directions on when to go ahead with the plan.

"Surely he wouldn't have gone ahead without my orders." Crandall whispered to himself. "I hadn't even paid him."

Convincing himself that he was not responsible the eminent surgeon climbed into his car and left for his clinic. Regardless the horrible man was dead and Sir Michael Crandall's secret was safe.

Jones and Smith were on their way to visit Cyril Blake at Club 54.

"Nasty piece of work this one," said Smith. "He came down from London in '38. Got himself in trouble with the Yard and had to move out of London. Unfortunately, he bought some of his associates with him. We know he dealt in the Black Market during the war and ran a betting syndicate up at the racetrack. There were also rumours that he ran high stake poker games, but he must have had someone tipping him off because we could never catch him red handed. He always seemed to know when we were planning a raid. Oh, we picked up some of his punters and sometimes took a long time to renew his liquor license but couldn't nail him for anything." Smith turned to Jones.

"Have you ever been inside his place?"

"No, it was always the uniform's territory so I'm looking forward to meeting this Mr. Blake."

The entrance to the club was off East Street, through Bartholomew's and then up a few back steps to a black door that was so well hidden probably only the club patrons and the police knew of its existence. Actually, the owners were very bold as the Club was only a short walk from the police station itself. Smith rapped smartly on the door and then turned the handle and walked in.

"Oiy we're not open yet get out" yelled a voice from the murky interior.

"Police here. Turn the lights on right now," ordered Jones.

"Oo the bloody hell do you think you are?" the voice grew louder as the man came towards them.

"Oh Sgt. didn't know it was you, why didn't you say so."

"This is Inspector Jones and we would like to speak with Cyril. I know he's in I spotted his car by the church."

"Just wait here Inspector and I'll go up and find him."

"No take us to him I want to have a good look around this place."

The man hurried across the floor switched on some overhead lights and tried to get up to the next floor before the officers, but they were at the office door just as he told the man behind the desk of their presence. The man didn't get up just muttered.

"What do you want Sgt. I aint got all day. I got a business to run yer know."

Jones strode across to the desk, slapped his warrant card on the blotter and calmly said,

"You will get on your feet and show me around this building unless you are prepared to be shut down."

Blake opened his mouth to protest, thought better of it and staggered to his feet.

"This way then." and led the officers through a series of rooms that were spread around three floors. He explained the so –called legitimate use of each room and ended the tour at the door where the officers had entered.

"I have some questions Mr. Blake. First of all, I need to see your membership list. Before you protest you can give it to me now or I will return with a search warrant for the entire building. Secondly do you, or allow anybody else to run gambling, betting or other illegal activities on your premises?"

"The list is in my desk. It's all proper and the members pay fifty pound a year to drink here"

"What is so special about drinking at this place when there are so many pubs around this area where they can drink without paying extra?" Blake looked up at Jones.

"Much better clientele, quieter and better mannered than pubs. My clients hold business meetings in some of the smaller rooms and as its men only they have peace from their nagging wives."

"What other kinds of meetings go on here?"

"I don't know what you mean Inspector." Was the brazen reply.

"I'll leave that for now but know that we are keeping an eye on these premises."

"Is that all?"

"No. I want you to look at this newspaper clipping from a few years ago and think back and remember who was involved in the scuffle."

"That's a long time ago. You can't expect me to remember that long."

"Yes, I do. According to our records it was a fight that started in the bar and ended out on the pavement."

"I remember now it was a new member, quite young, who said that another member had insulted him and so he took a swing at him."

"Who was the other man?" Blake looked hard at the Inspector.

"I can't remember, really I can't" the man whined.

"Who was the investigative officer?"

"I can't remember that either."

Jones took a couple of steps closer to the worried looking Blake.

"I find it unusual that you can remember some things but not others. Do you always have such a selective memory Mr. Blake?"

Turning to Smith Jones called, "Sgt. call back to the station and make preparations to close this place down. I have lost patience with Mr. Blake."

As Smith moved towards the outside door Blake spoke up.

"No wait. I can remember now. The other man was that ponsy actor. He and his friends often came in here but that night, it was a Saturday, and he was alone. Then he started onto the young man."

"What do you mean 'started onto the young man?"

"You know he was chatting him up like those kinds of men do?"

"What kind of men?" asked Jones looking straight into Blake's eyes.

"You know those homo fellows."

"What was this older man's name? "

"Davies, Martin I think but he's not living down here anymore. I heard he got steady work in Bournemouth."

"And the officer?"

"That was Sgt. Bloody Blount- he was a right bastard. Always wanting money to look the other way. I paid him for I 'eard someone did 'im is that right Inspector. 'E was bad, but I wouldn't swing for him. For sure."

"How well did you know Blount?"

"Well enough to keep out of his way. But I didn't do 'im Inspector, I just paid him for information whenever he came in."   By now Cyril Blake was pleading with Jones.

"Okay, that's it for now Mr. Blake but remember we are watching you." And with that warning the officers left Club 54.

"Our list of suspects grows Sgt. and we haven't completely solved all the files yet. All of them wanted him out of their lives but who is capable not only of the killing but also the dismemberment?"

"I don't think we are looking for somebody who will murder again. I think this murder is one of revenge and was committed in a calculated and premeditated manner. What do you think Sir?"

"Absolutely. We have nothing to fear from this person and when found will probably behave in a very calm, rational and logical manner."

The two officers reached the steps of the station.

"It's the weekend," said Jones. "You and I are going to spend a quiet two days doing whatever we want. I know you want to watch your boy play soccer tomorrow and I have plans for tomorrow evening. I know that both Jenkins and Masters are off but Atkinson isn't so he can spend time tracking down that actor, Martin Davies. Then first thing Monday will try to finish up the interviews and hopefully be able to narrow our list of suspects down."

After clearing off his desk Jones left the station and took his usual route home to his flat in Palmeria Square. He had a car but preferred to use it only for trips out exploring the Sussex and Hampshire countryside. Walking was his preferred mode of transport and when he had the time, he would spend many hours walking the public paths across the South Downs enjoying the panoramic view out to the English Channel. Many parts of Brighton and the coastal areas showed the scars of war but looking down from the Downs they were hidden amongst the other buildings and became part of the natural landscape. On a clear day he could see across the Channel almost to France and then he would sit on the grass always surprised to realize how close the war had really been.

CHAPTER FOURTEEN

The green room was empty the other actors were on earlier than him so he could digest this news by himself. Davies had never told anyone about his business with Blount. He had thought about bringing it to an end by reporting Blount to the police, but he was never sure enough that he would be believed or even listened to. He was well aware that a homosexual man was not seen as a credible complainant in any walk of life. Davies had contemplated going to Australia or even America but always drew back knowing that he would be giving up a reasonably well-paid niche in London to start from the beginning, with neither friends nor family to support him. Now he knew he was free. But who had killed Blount?

"Who cares!" he said as he stood up and flung the colourful scarf around his neck, "It wasn't me, but ding-dong, the beast is gone," sang Davies as he left the dressing room almost waltzing to side stage readying himself for his opening entrance

Jones arrived early at his desk on Monday morning. His weekend had gone well and now he was raring to go and get the murder of Blount finished with. But even this early he was still behind Supt. Young who had just left, on Jones' desk, a comprehensive list of present and past officers who may have had a working relationship with Blount. The list was long but Young had clearly marked the status of each officer and for the current officers had pencilled in an appointment time for that day. Young had even left telephone numbers and addresses for those officers who had retired. The list was so thorough that even former officers who had died but had known Blount were noted. Jones knew that his Supt. was as anxious as he to get this case resolved and put away. The thoroughness of this list spoke to the Supt's need to help Jones to get this matter dealt with.

The other memo on his blotter was from Atkinson. The constable had been able to track down Martin Davies through a London Agency and found that currently Davies was appearing at Drury Lane, in the West End.

Smith arrived at Jones' office with WPC Jenkins who had her final report on the missing files. Jenkins had matched up the numbers on the individual sheets with the money deposited in the Littlehampton bank account. The amounts from Mrs. Ainslee and Mr. Palmer balanced with the sheets as did the initials, dates and amount for Martin Davies. Jenkins pointed out the deposits that had come to an end.

"As they stopped before, in some cases a year before, he was killed it could be that the victim died or left the country. But we have three active files that still have money going in, but I haven't been able to match them with an incident or a report of an incident or anything that we know up to now."

"Did you unravel most of the codes?"

"Yes, we have the date and amount of money, but we have only the initials of the victims."

"Thanks Jenkins. While you are here, I don't think I have ever asked you if you knew Blount."

"No sir, I came in just after he had left. I knew of him by what I heard being said in the canteen but nothing definite Sir."

"Sgt. the Super has left me this list of men covering the years that Blount was here can you go over it for me and make contact with the retired men to see who worked closely with Blount. As you can see the interviews here begin at 10.00am can you be finished by then?"

"I'll do my best," said Smith already walking out of the door.

Jones took another look at the files comparing them with one another. The difference in the amounts of payments interested him; obviously one of the victims was much richer than the other two and had been paying for five years.

"Perhaps a professional man" speculated Jones. The next largest amount had been going in for three years but strangely the smallest amount had been paid for almost six.

The morning interviews produced very little new information about Blount. It soon became very obvious that those men who had worked with him did not like his methods and quickly asked for transfers to other squads. Others spoke of his ill temper with civilians and his morose manner around the station. When asked about which constable spent the majority of time with Blount two names popped up one was

Baker, a detective constable who was with Blount when Blount first started at Brighton. But Baker signed up in '40 and nobody had heard from him since. The second name to show up was that of Waters, another detective constable who like Baker had left the force. It was thought that Waters had gone abroad as soon as the war ended, either to Canada or Australia.

"It looks as though Waters is the man we need to speak to as his employment dates match up with the majority of the files."

"Yes, and remember Mrs. Ainslee spoke of a Waters being with Blount and Mrs. Palmer said there were two officers as did our friend at the club. But how do we get hold of him? "wondered Smith. "His former Supt. McLeod, is dead, but his former Inspector is still in this area, his address is on Supt Young's list. Yes, here he is living in Rottingdean. I hadn't got down to him. Shall I call him?"

"Yes, but make an appointment for later this afternoon I think he would be more helpful if we went out to him. What do you think?" Five minutes later Smith was back with a meeting set for 3.30 that afternoon.

Jones' phone rang, "Dr. Marshall here. You requested details on a William Palmer who was drowned out near Ditchling. According to my report he was pulled out at approximately 9.00 pm on that Sunday but given the state of the body I estimated time of death at least five hours before that."

"How does that compare with the time of death of Blount?"

"As you know I can only give you an approximation of Blount's time of death, but that period would include Palmer's. It certainly was within a few days of Blount's but whether before or afterwards it's difficult to say given the condition of Blount. I'm sorry I can't help you Dai."

"Okay thanks doc." Jones walked down to Smith's office.

"No luck on getting a definite time connection between the deaths of Blount and Palmer so we'll have to go back to the money and see when Palmer put in his last payment. Will you assign that?"

"Of course. I'll just be five minutes and then we'll go to Rottingdean?"

The drive to Rottingdean was only ten minutes but it was along the coastal road that gave a panoramic view of the Channel with its boats bringing their trade from Europe and Scandinavia to the many ports along the Southern shore. The green of the water contrasted sharply with the whiteness of the chalky cliffs that began just east of Brighton and stretched along the coast to the busy port of Dover.

"You must know Inspector Steele quite well Jack?"

"I was never in his squad, but I know that he was a fair boss and interested in how his men were doing. Apparently, he was a good man when anybody had work or home difficulties. I do remember one time when one of his constables lost a brother in a road accident. Even when we were so shorthanded Steele fixed the schedule so that the constable could spend several days with his parents. He himself is a widower, his wife died several years back. I believe his children are all moved away now."

Owen Steele's bungalow was set back a little from the coast road and nestled into the foot of the Downs. There was a small but well-maintained front garden and a crazy-paving path that led to a light brown front door which opened as the men walked up the path.

"Good to see you again Jack. How 've you been keeping?"

"Nice to see you too, Owen. You look very well".

"Certainly can't complain," the tall grey-haired man replied. "Come on in."

Smith made the introductions and the three men sat down in the comfortably furnished large room from which could be seen both the Channel to the south and Downs to the north.

"Would you like tea? I can get it."

"No thanks, "said Jones. "We'll just sit here and enjoy the view while we talk."

"I knew you would be out to see me soon," said the older man. "After reading about Ray Blount I pictured the back checking you would have to do and that eventually my name would come up. I bet the C.C. is not handling this very well. I remember what it was like to have that particular man on my back. Any clues yet about who did it or why?"

"We think we have a handle on why. Our investigations have led us to several people who were being blackmailed by Blount. Some of the cases go back five years. We have found his bank accounts which show he received regular monthly payments spanning seven years. We have been able to decode and match victims with incidents and some of Blount's files but there are several files we cannot find any connection at all."

"How many viable suspects do you have?"

"Perhaps three, but we're still unable to connect any of them with the Steyning location."

"I always felt Blount was a bad lot and that Newcastle had done us a dirty deal, but it was never possible to get real evidence against him. Anyway, how can I help?"

"Two things; firstly, can you remember any cases or incidents connected with Blount that surprised you when they were not pursued further and secondly do you know of the whereabouts of Detective Constable Waters?"

"Ah yes Waters. He was a smart young constable and I was very sorry that he left the Force. I remember he hated working with Blount but during those times it was difficult to match up compatible men. He did make several complaints about Blount, but nothing went anywhere, and I know that was part of his frustration and why he left."

"Do you know where he is now?"

"Yes, he is in Canada; He joined up with the Mounties as soon as he could. He had a sister out there already who offered him a place to stay. I have an old address for him, a place called Moose Jaw, but he wrote that he was going on a tour of duty further north and would send me his new address. But it hasn't arrived yet."

"Can you remember any of those incidents that Waters spoke to you about?"

"No, not offhand but let me think about it and I'll call you tomorrow. I'll also look up his last letter; he always sends one or two letters a year. Apparently, all of his immediate family are out in Canada now and I'm his only contact with the old country."

"Thanks for your help Inspector and we'll hear from you tomorrow," said Jones rising to leave.

"Just give me time I'll remember something. Goodbye Inspector. Goodbye Jack perhaps you'll visit again now you know where I am."

"I'll try, good to see you Owen."

On the way back to the office the policeman debated the best way to get hold of Constable Waters. Finally, they decided that first thing in the morning Jones would be put in a call to Canada House in London and seek advice on how to reach Waters.

CHAPTER FIFTEEN

Their arrival at the Newcastle Police station was not met with enthusiasm. Supt. Young had called the previous day to check that his counterpart was back after being on sick leave and as he was Young confirmed that he and his officers would be at Newcastle station to discuss the Blount case with him. But on arrival the three Sussex men were met by a very young constable, taken to the canteen and left while the young constable went to fetch the Super. Half an hour later they were still sitting there with their empty teacups. Young clambered to his feet exclaiming to the entire canteen.

"This is totally unacceptable," and strode out of the canteen down the hallway to the front desk.

"Who is in charge of this station?" Young thundered at the desk Sgt.

"Err Supt. Crump is the senior Supt. Sir."

"Alright where is Supt. Crump?"

"I don't know sir."

"Then find him. And be quick about it."

Young's face was growing increasingly puce-coloured and both Jones and Smith knew what that meant and were very pleased to stand back and watch their Supt. in action. Within minutes they heard the clattering footsteps of the returning clerk hurrying towards them.

"Well," barked Young.

"Supt. Crump is just finishing his lunch in his office and said he'll be with you as soon as he has finished his correspondence."

"Really. Then it's going to be sooner that he thinks. Lead the way son." They all noticed that the desk Sgt. had quietly slipped out of sight leaving the civilian clerk to cope.

"I can't do that. He specifically said that I wasn't to take you to his office."

"Alright just show us the way and you can return to your duties here."

By now Young's face had gone from puce to white. The Sussex men had seen this degree of anger before and knew that Young had reached the limit of his patience. The officers were led to a bend in the corridor where the clerk silently pointed out the third door on the left and promptly vanished. Young turned to his men.

"Ready for the charge."

He knocked sharply on the door and strode through without waiting for an invitation. The large man seated at his desk looked up at the intrusion, but Young didn't hesitate.

"Good afternoon Superintendent Crump, I am Superintendent Young, this is Inspector Jones and Sergeant Smith of the Sussex Constabulary and we are here as promised to discuss the murder of former Sgt. Blount who served with this station until he came down to us."

"I am just finishing my lunch," the man feebly protested.

"Yes I can see that but there must have been some mix-up at this end as we have been here over half an hour and as a fellow senior officer we knew that you would be embarrassed if we were kept waiting any longer."

Already embarrassed the man began to bluster about not being told about their visit. But Young interjected, "There does seem to be a breakdown in communications as we were told that you had been informed about our visit. But we are here now and would like to begin our meeting."

As the three men pulled up chairs and seated themselves around his desk Supt. Crump cleared away the remains of his lunch and then telephoned for his Chief Inspector of Detectives to come to the meeting.

"Immediately, then find him and get him here now," was his frantic message to whoever answered the call.

Supt. Young leaned across and whispered something to Smith who nodded and quietly left the room. Within minutes a tall, lean man entered the room and was introduced, with visible relief, by Crump, as C.I. Farley. Once introductions were completed Young began by explaining the circumstances of the murder and the need for more information on Blount's background. Crump was very fidgety during Young's explanation and as soon as Young had finished Crump got up saying that he was sure Inspector Farley could provide all the information they needed and that he had urgent work to do.

But the man from Sussex was not to be fobbed off so quickly and he reminded Crump that it was his signature, as the supervising Inspector, who had written and signed Blount's application for a transfer to Sussex.

"And you wrote him a glowing recommendation," added Young waving the form at Crump who reluctantly sat back down at his desk.

"Sgt. Blount was a hard worker who always did more of his share of extra duty. He participated in the social side of the station and he needed to move for personal reasons. It's all written there," was Crump's feeble response, never once looking up from his desk.

"What were the personal reasons he gave?" asked Jones

"Oh, his wife was not happy and wanted to move south to be closer to her family."

"But putting those personal reasons to one side, your Sgt. Blount was trouble. The personal reasons had nothing to do with the problems he was causing here. His bullying of citizens, his abruptness with colleagues, and the complaints received here about his rudeness and lack of respect for authority. None of those things had any bearing on his wish to transfer?"

Young spoke calmly keeping his eyes firmly fixed on Crump's face. The man shuffled papers on his desk as he sought, unsuccessfully, to find a credible answer to Young's accusations.

But Young went on. "While investigating Blount's record I found this report in his file. It is a record of a conversation between two of your men and two from our station who met up during a course at Bletchley."

He showed the second report to Crump and gave a copy to Farley.

"It is very unusual for officers to complain about colleagues but as you can see both of your men felt strongly enough to allow their names to be used. So now let's put an end to all this avoidance of the real issue and tell me about Blount. And why you sent him to us. Well I am waiting for an explanation."

Crump fidgeted in his seat, he looked across at Farley mentally pleading with him to help him out, but the Chief Inspector had his head down engrossed in the papers on his lap. Hesitantly Crump started and then crumbled.

"Yes, Blount was a troublemaker and he was all that you say he was. But he was more, he was always working on what he called his schemes. We found out that he took bribes for looking the other way for traffic incidents. He took money from publicans who served alcohol after hours and from those who ran betting syndicates. We could never gather enough concrete evidence to nail him as people were too afraid that he would harm them if they spoke up. But one day a citizen laid a serious complaint against him and we had to act. As you said I was his Inspector then and this was my chance to get rid of him. But given the uncertainty of the times and the expected shortage of experienced policeman I wasn't allowed to sack him. So, I sent him to you," he finished lamely.

"Well, at least we now have confirmation that Blount was always a bad lot, no wonder his wife left him, "remarked Jones.

"That's why he went. The complaint against him was laid by a citizen who, along with a couple of other actually saw Blount hit his wife."

"Well you certainly sent us a bundle of trouble and now that he is dead, and in such a manner, we have to uncover all the information we can. You know it is possible that his murderer came from up here. Obviously, he had enemies here too. I would like to speak with any officer who went out with him. I realize it is a few years ago but we need that information."

A very resigned Supt. Crump gestured to his officer and it became obvious that the visit by the Sussex officers had been expected as Inspector Farley not only had Blount's record of employment he also had a short list of the men who had been associated with Blount.

"Blount was promoted after just a few years with us and I have the names of three detective constables who partnered with Blount. The earliest was Edward Adams he was with Blount for four years, then he transferred to the Birmingham Force for a couple of years. We heard that he had signed up in the R.A.F and unfortunately was killed. The next man was Colin Alexander who was with Blount through the next two years, unfortunately he was killed in a
very tragic hit and run. There were suspicions that Blount was behind it as Alexander had put in three complaints about Blount. But we couldn't prove anything. The last partner was Derek Bond, he was very helpful in

getting evidence against Blount, but he was badly injured out with Montgomery and never came back to us. Last we heard of him was that he was down your way at St. Dunstan's. We do know he had family home in Scotland." Crump handed over the records to Jones asking,

"Is there anything else that you want?"

"Yes. We want a list of all Blount's cases where charges were laid, and a prison sentence resulted. Although the crime was committed on our patch it is quite reasonable to think that the perpetrator was known to Blount before he arrived down South."

Inspector Farley handed Jones a thin brown file.

"Here are the case files. I have noted those that are still incarcerated and those who have been released are listed along with their latest address. You will find that some are deceased while there are a few that we haven't been able to track down at all."

Jones   casually flipped through the file and then asked both Newcastle officers if there was any case that involved Blount in particular and gave then cause for concern.

"No," instantly answered Crump, every case was properly handled and proven."

Farley glanced quickly at his Superintend and then looked at his feet. Young and Jones conferred realizing that they had just about all they were going to get from these men. Thanking Crump and Farley for their assistance and promising to keep them informed as the case progressed the men from Sussex left heading back to the front desk and Sgt Smith.

"Yes, there's a nice-looking restaurant down in the Square "Smith said in answer to Young's enquiry about getting a meal.

Once settled with their fish and chips the three men began to summarize their information. Jones went quickly through the meeting with Supt. Crump showing Smith the documentation that had been provided and commenting about the irony that all three of Blount's former partners had not returned to the Force.

"When we get back to Brighton, we could send Masters out to St. Dunstan's to check out this Derek Bond. Masters is quite an empathetic young man and might just be able to coax more out of this Bond chap," suggested Smith.

Young wanted to know what Smith had discovered on his prowl around the station. Both Young and Jones fully appreciated Smith's ability to put people at their ease by being friendly and a good listener. Much of what he learned was confirmation of previous information but in speaking to some of the older men Smith had been given the name of a retired sergeant who, as an almost permanent front desk officer, would know much more about what Blount was up to. It was a known fact that front desk officers were the most valuable source about the activities in any station.

Smith added "I took the liberty of calling him from the station and he agreed to see us whenever we are free. He says he is in the rest of the day and we could just go around. I have directions to his home. It's just ten minutes away"

"Okay" agreed Young, "We'll just finish up here and then see if we can learn anything new from the Sgt."

As promised their journey was short and soon they were settled in a well maintained and comfortably furnished red brick terraced house. Sgt. Scott was a large man and his shabby but comfortable clothes contrasted vividly with the brightly coloured furniture and expensive ornaments placed around the room.

"Welcome to Newcastle. I heard you were coming up today and I wanted to be sure that we met as I spent twenty years on that front desk and there wasn't much I didn't know."

"Well that's a nice change," said Jones "We were treated as if we had the plague at the station."

"Yes, the senior men were frightened of what you'd found out. That Supt. Crump is frightened by his own shadow. If it wasn't for the shortage of men after the war he would never have got to that position. Filling dead men's shoes-that's how he got that job."

"Not high on your list of respected colleagues then?" asked Smith.

"No indeed. When he was Blount's Inspector he would never stand up to Blount. He let Blount get away with murder. Literally. Many of us were sure that Blount arranged that little traffic accident that killed young Colin. And what did Mr. Crump do? He put Blount in charge of the investigation and naturally the investigation went nowhere. Bloody shame that."

"We have information on Blount's activities after he left our Force which could be the motive, but we are having difficulty linking up those possibilities with the location of the body. I am wondering if you knew of anybody linked to Blount who had connections down south and would know that area of Sussex?"

"Most of the men have moved on now, some have died as I mentioned some went abroad looking for a better life but many left the force but stayed up north, going into the heavy factories that started up quickly after '45,"explained Scott.

"What about his own family?" asked Supt. Young, "did you know where he came from?"

"Yes, he originally came from Manchester. By the sound of it he had a rough upbringing. His mum died early and after a while his dad remarried and according to Blount the new wife was cruel. She beat Blount, and wouldn't let him eat until he had done all the chores around the house and even then he wasn't allowed up at the table with the others. It was she who made him leave home when he was thirteen, with very little schooling."

"How did he get on the Force then?"

"He went to work in a ceramics factory and an older man took pity on him and took him into his home and taught him how to read and write properly. Then supported him while he took courses at night school until he passed the Police exam. It was a blessing that the old man passed away soon after Blount got into the Force and started up to his tricks."

"Was Blount always angry about things?"

"When he came to us, he had a real chip on his shoulder and was determined to take what he could out of life. Even if it meant hurting others."

"That certainly gives up a better picture of Blount as a young man. Anybody up here that you think would have reason to kill Blount?"

"Well I did hear that some of the convictions were based on suspect evidence supplied by Blount. But as for our people as I said most men have gone one way or another and once Blount himself was gone down south things settled down."

Jones opened his briefcase and pulled out a file. "Inspector Farley gave me this list of Blount's cases but when I asked if there was anything notable about any of them both he and Supt. Crump said no."

"If I could see the list it would jog my memory. If you don't mind sir."

Jones passed over the list and waited as the former Sgt. put on his glasses and looked down the columns.

"Here's one that was suspicious. Young Donny Harrison was in trouble all through his young life. Shoplifting, stealing petrol and a bit of B. and B. but nothing much really. We all knew Donny. He had a tough young life and sometimes we thought he did his crime so that he could come here and be with us. But Blount had it in for him and pulled him in for assault with a deadly weapon, claiming that Donny had attacked a passer-by with a knife."

"And had he?" asked Jones.

"Well he had been in a fight and was bruised about the face, but he said his dad did that. Unfortunately, when he was searched a small knife was found in his coat pocket, but Donny swore up and down that it wasn't his. We tended to believe him as we'd never known Donny to carry a weapon. But the other fellow laid a charge and with Blount's evidence the lad was put away for almost seven years. I don't know if he is out yet. We heard at the station that he was given a rough time in prison."

"Is that the only suspicious one on the list?"

"Well it was the worst one." Scott went down the list, "This man was sent down for six months but he's out of course and took one of those cheap trips to Australia. He's long gone. This one, Blackstone, he was a nasty customer, a local builder who according to Blount was caught red handed stealing supplies from the back of lorries. He went down for three years and was out by the time Blount left Newcastle. Blackstone met an Irish girl who settled him down and now they are doing well over there. Still in the building trade. He was very angry when he came out, but she persuaded him to let the past go. There was a rumour that somehow Blount had messed with the evidence, but nothing was proven."

"No one else?"

"Not really. I should say that Donny was the most likely, but he was never a violent lad here, but one never knows what happened to him in prison. Try him but I would be most surprised if he was your man. This was his address, but I haven't seen him since he went away. Scott passed the paper back to Jones.

"Course I never heard what happened to Blount's stepsister did you?"

All three men looked up startled.

"What stepsister?" Smith finally got out.

"When his father remarried the woman already had a daughter who was about ten years older than the boy, and by all accounts she was even worse than the stepmother, bullying Ray and always getting him into trouble and getting him whipped. Blount had some idea that she was down south working in service, but he didn't know where. He said he wasn't interested in making contact with her. He was fine by himself and did seem happier once he was married."

After leaving the Sgt's house the three men sat in the car and digested the latest information on Blount.

"Obviously the fact that Blount had a sister never came up in our investigation. We'll have to track her down although with the publicity that this case has had one would think she would have come forward by now," said Jones.

"Yes, we must find her, if she is still alive. She was about ten years older so that would make her about late fifties. But we have no idea what her last name was, if she has married, we are even further in the dark with her name," added Smith.

"We also have to trace this Donny Harrison," added Jones.

It had been his plan to find somewhere to stay just outside of London and then drive into the West End and interview Martin Davies but now he was having second thoughts and wanted to get home tonight so that he could get an early start the next day. It was decided that they would drop Smith off at a small hotel by Victoria Station while they would head back to Brighton. Smith would interview Davies the next morning and then return by train.

Once settled in his room Smith started to record all the known facts of the case. As much as he respected his Inspector, Smith felt that the investigation needed to concentrate more on the actual murder. It was proper that all of the known players had to be interviewed if only to discard them as suspects but so far nobody, in Smith's estimation, seemed a likely murderer. Smith instinctively felt that a parallel investigation into Steyning and what happened both in Baxter House and in the village would yield new information. Smith always believed that the eyes and ears of ordinary people were the best information gathering method in detecting crime and that was especially true in the smaller villages. With that in mind Smith drew up a list of approaches and questions to take back to Steyning. One thing that Smith was sure of was that Blount having a car like the silver sports one found in his lockup, was the type of man who would be driving it around the countryside. Probably would take it to the country pubs for a Sunday morning drink simply to show it off. Smith was also convinced that placing the body in Baxter House was no coincidence but rather it was a place chosen because of its connection to the murderer and probably even to Blount himself.

As a young policeman Smith had been quite content to be a foot slogger a beat policeman looking after his particular section of the community. But like tens of thousands of other men the war intervened in their plans and for Smith it was a move to fill the vacant position of Detective Sergeant.

When Jones came aboard Smith was apprehensive about how this young, well-connected policeman would react to the rather comfortable routines and processes that Smith had introduced. But now after working together on several complicated cases Smith had come to appreciate the younger man's grasp of the important values of being a policeman. Jones had made changes but always with Smith's input and each change had bought about a greater efficiency in internal communications and better use of personnel.

"But," thought Smith as he climbed into bed, "I still believe that the answer to Blount's murder lies in Steyning or close by."

He plumped his pillow and said goodnight to Helen as he fell asleep.

CHAPTER SIXTEEN

Smith arrived back at the station in the early afternoon and reported to Jones that Martin Davies appeared to have a watertight alibi for the period of Blount's murder. According to corroborating witnesses Davies was up in Edinburgh doing a month-long pre-West End performance with the current cast.

"I was assured that nobody had time to leave Edinburgh as they gave two shows a day and were at rehearsals every morning and our Mr. Davies had the leading male role. I did speak at length to Davies and confirmed that he was being blackmailed by Blount and that he made payments regularly each month. Apparently, Blount would telephone Davies and it didn't matter where Davies was playing Blount would go and pick up the cash at some local pub."

"Did he know Blount was dead?"

"Oh yes and he was thrilled about it, He actually told me that he thought about doing for Blount himself but always seemed to be too busy. Funny bloke actually but I would never consider him to be our murderer."

"I'm glad to hear that Sgt now let's go down to the Super's office, we were waiting for you. We are going to discuss frankly our thoughts on this case and review what we have so far. You're feeling about Davies gives us a good start."

Just as they turned the corner leading to the conference room Jones and Smith were waylaid by Supt. Young.

"Sorry Dai but the C.C. has turned up and wants to listen in to our discussion. And he has invited the A.C.C. to accompany him!"

Supt. Young was obviously angry at the change of arrangements and the short notice given to Jones for preparation. But he need not have worried as Inspector Jones was well prepared and confident that he could answer all questions thrown at him. Jones and the Chief Constable seldom saw eye to eye, but he had never been able to fault Jones on procedural matters, much to the C.C.'s dismay.

Jones hung several charts over the blackboard as the men settled themselves around the table. Jones looked across at Young and winked letting his Super know that he wasn't at all bothered by the presence of the senior men and was confident of the process so far.

"I have divided this investigation into three sections as per the charts in front of you." Pointing to the first one Jones continued. "This one deals with matters before Blount came to us, both his personal background and his time in Newcastle. This second one deals with his time here in Sussex and this last one deals with his activities since his dismissal and of course his subsequent murder. I will deal with each section separately having discussion before moving to the next. Any questions?"

"Oh, get on with man I don't have all day you know I am a busy man, things to do you know," grumbled the C.C.

Smith looked out of the window trying his best to hide a smile. Both he and Jones anticipated that the two senior men would join the meeting. It had become a habit of the C.C. to sit in at this stage of any investigation and haggle over bits of minutiae that seldom helped the investigation along. Now it would seem that the Assistant C.C. was always to accompany him but as his total responsibility was the Uniform branch all he ever offered was a series of opinions on the investigative process. His comments didn't appear to worry Jones, but Smith had often seen Superintendent Young squirming in his chair as he felt the competency of his detectives was being questioned.

Concisely Jones worked his way through all the information that they had regarding Blount's stay in Newcastle, listing each name and that person's connection to the case. At the bottom of the chart Jones had listed the next steps to be taken: tracking down Derek Bond, a former colleague of Blount and Donny Harrison an apparent victim of Blount and finally Blount's stepsister.

Moving on to the middle chart Jones described the finding of Blount's current address, and of the storage unit and its contents. He explained how PW Jenkins had cracked the code on Blount's files although not all the victims had been identified. Those victims they did know had been interviewed and they were sure that Martin Davies, William Palmer and Mrs. Ainslee were not suspects.

"What?" exploded the CC. "Are you telling me that you went out to see Mrs. Palmer even though her husband had so recently passed away in such tragic circumstances? How ridiculous, as if that poor woman didn't have enough to deal with. You should have checked with me I could have told you neither she nor her husband would have any connection with such a blaggard as Blount."

The Chief Constable snapped his swagger stick on the table to emphasize his anger. Jones took a moment and then reminded everyone that at the time Blount came into contact with the Palmers he was a member of the Sussex Police Force legitimately investigating a boy's death and that as a result of Blount's work Mr. Palmer agreed to become a blackmail victim rather than confess to running the boy down and leaving him to die.

It was tense in the conference room as all eyes were averted from the snorting and puffing C.C. Suddenly, he stood up saying that he had heard enough and would not stay further. Both he and his ACC quickly withdrew from the meeting leaving a relieved trio to plan the next steps in finding Blount's killer.

It has been two weeks since I killed the monster. I have no regrets. He deserved what he got, and I am sure that I am not the only person that he tormented. Now they can share in my relief that he is gone. I did the world a favour by getting rid of an animal- he was never good enough to be called a man. Displaying him in pieces was a masterpiece. I felt that was fittingly symbolic of the way he would continually tear strips from my life. I wanted him to be displayed in the most humiliating position possible so when the police came, they'd understand how wicked he had been. When I look back on that day, I am proud of how careful I was to not to leave any clues about my identity. I certainly wanted him discovered and it has given me a great deal pleasure to know that he was found as I left him. The police are making their enquiries, but they have no reason to suspect me. I have been so careful, but I must maintain my composure and carry on as usual until the police give up.

It was a couple of days later that Smith heard from Owen Steel. After customary small talk was exchanged Steel told Smith what he had remembered.

"It was something to do with a doctor who ran a clinic in Hove. The house was at the top end of Dyke Road, one of those houses set well back off the road. Anyway, a young man came into the station one day and wanted to lay criminal charges against the doctor and the clinic. It seems his younger sister had gone to the clinic for treatment and two days later she was dead. Now the brother thinks his sister was pregnant, early stages, but the death certificate said the girl died of pneumonia." Steel paused for breath. "Apparently the brother suspected his sister was in trouble as she had called him twice the day before just to chat, which was very unusual according to the brother. Anyway, next thing he knew was that his father called to say his sister had died at the clinic. I remember him coming into the station, he was so upset and demanded that something be done. Inspector McLeod passed the case over to Blount and we heard no more. Some of us asked around to see what had had happened but our questions were brushed off by Blount." He paused and Smith waited.

"Another one I remembered was about a scuffle outside Club 54 on East Street. Blount went out to investigate and came back saying it was nothing *'a bunch of fags getting their knickers in a twist'* were his actual words. That went away too. Although I believe that Waters was on that one with Blount. Anyway, that's about all I can remember about specific cases. I do know that many citizens actually came to the station looking for Blount. They used to say it was a *'private matter'* and wouldn't talk to anyone else."

Smith thanked his former colleague for the new information and promised to be out to see him in a couple of weeks.

D. C. Masters had been given the job of tracking down former D.C. Waters now of the Royal Canadian Mounted Police.

"It was a tricky business," he explained to Smith. "First of all, I went to Canada House, who gave me the details to contact the R.C.M.P. at their headquarters in Regina. I did that and was put through to a Captain Pellam who then gave me a number for the Moose Jaw contingent. When I finally got through to them a Constable Peterson explained that Waters was out on assignment up north and would be away for two weeks. He, Peterson, gave me a number for the substation that Waters reported into every day. Apparently, he can report in by radio and if it's urgent they can get him back to the station more quickly. But the weather can be extreme where he is, so we'll just have to try our luck. He reports in about 6 o'clock in the evening their time, which is about midnight our time. Inspector Pellam said that he would coordinate a call if we would give him the day and time. I guess it's pretty remote out there in northern Saskatchewan."

It was mid- afternoon three days later when the call from Canada came in. Waters explained that a case had bought him into the office that day and it seemed a good time to call the U.K. It didn't take long for Jones to verify that Waters was indeed Blount's partner and to explain about Blount's murder and the ensuring investigation. Waters had not heard anything but was more than ready to talk about his time with Blount. Jones explained that they knew about the dress shop burglary, the scuffle at Club 54 and the headmaster at Ditchling and a few other victims who were either dead or had left the country.

"There were quite a few that Blount had his fist into besides those you have mentioned. Can I have a day to think about this and I will send a report tomorrow into Inspector Pellam at Headquarters. Would that be okay?'

Jones agreed to wait for the extra day but before he let Waters go, he asked him why he left the Sussex Constabulary.

"Well sir nobody wanted to nail Blount despite the complaints that were laid by myself and other men and I couldn't see a future for me working with senior men who didn't care enough and would rather see the reputation of the station pulled down by a rotten copper like Blount than stand up to him."

"Well I'm sorry that you had to move so far away but I look forward to hearing your report and hopefully it will have something that can move us closer to catching the killer. Thanks for calling. Goodbye."

Jones had hardly replaced the receiver when the telephone rang again.

"Sgt. Hewitt here sir, from Steyning. I thought you should know that young Stuart Hughes is here in Steyning. He has been here a couple of days visiting a girlfriend. One of my constables spotted him going into the local grocery shop. But he is at her house now."

"Thanks Sgt. We will be out there as soon as we can. Please put a watch on him and detain if he looks like leaving the area."

"Will do that. By the way he is now in the R.A.F. so probably on leave. I will go over to the house now."

The ride out to Steyning provided Smith with another opportunity to push forward his ideas about deeper investigations into the Steyning connection. Yesterday both Jones and Young had listened to Smith's suggestions, but no decision had been made.

"What if you stayed out here for a couple of days," said Jones. "I do understand what you mean, and your instincts have never led us astray. You spend two or three days here mixing with the locals and call in every day. How about that?" suggested Jones.

"I will drive my own car out here and apart from the Estate agents I haven't had very much contact with the locals so that should be good for information or gossip," agreed Smith.

CHAPTER SEVENTEEN

Stuart Hughes was a good looking, dark haired, rather tall young man who wore his RAF uniform very proudly. At first, he was reluctant to answer questions about his life at Baxter House and was even more so to tell why he was back in Steyning now or earlier in the spring. Finally, he explained to Jones that his time at Baxter House was not a happy one. His parents had been bombed out of their London house and their eldest daughter, his sister, had died as a result of injuries suffered that night.

"They came down here thinking it would be safe for me, but I hated it here. It was so quiet, and the local boys had their own groups and wouldn't let me in because they said I talked funny. I had to leave all my friends in London. I was in a football team and we played every Saturday. It didn't matter if the bombers came, we used to hide in the trees and then go back to the game. It was great fun. I really wanted to stay with my pals, their parents agreed to look after me, but Mum wouldn't hear of it. So, we came here but there was nothing for me to do, except scrump a few apples now and again. And Mum and Dad were so unhappy they just dragged themselves about the house. I know I shouldn't blame them, but I missed my sister too and I had nobody to talk to."

"But later you did find a sweetheart though?" interjected Smith.

"Yes, Brenda and I went to school together, we were in the same form and she was the only girl who paid any attention to me, the outsider."

"You didn't want to go with your parents to Australia then?"

"No, I had made contact with my old mates from London and we all decided that when our time came, we would all do our National Service in the RAF. Mum and Dad were very sad people, never got over my sister's death I suppose. But dad had a brother out there so that's what they decided to do."

"Well we won't keep you long, but we need to ask you a couple of questions. You do admit to being back here in the past spring. Why?"

"I came back to see if I could see Brenda. My squadron had been told that we were going to Singapore later this year and all my mates had girlfriends or sisters who promised to write to them so I hoped that perhaps Brenda would write to me. That's why I came down."

"Did you visit Baxter House that day?"

"Yes, I did. Brenda had gone shopping with her mum, so I had time to kill so I went back to see some of the old places. I saw the Board up at the house, so I went in and looked around. Some of that furniture belonged to my parents you know."

"How did you get in?"

"Oh, that was easy, through the underground tunnel that goes from the summer shed to the kitchen. I always went that way when I wanted to sneak in or out of the house."

"Did you see anything unusual in the house?"

"Only all the dust sheets and the place smelled stale and old. But nothing special. Why are you asking these questions? I know about the body but what's that got to do with me. It wasn't there when I had a look 'round. I didn't kill anybody. Our squadron did six straight weeks of training and I didn't leave the camp until a couple of days ago. Besides I don't have a car, can't drive yet, so how could I have got out here and back before anybody noticed. Besides that, I didn't know that policeman. The only coppers I knew were Sgt. Hewitt and the constable who's been following me around today."

Sgt. Smith pulled out a photograph. "Do you know this man?" he asked. Hughes took his time answering and turned the photo to see at different angles.

"I don't know who he is, but I have seen him before. Is he the copper?" Smith nodded.

"Well he wasn't in uniform I would have remembered sooner. Tough looking man. No, he was in the church car park, not here, up over at Ditchling church. He was speaking with an old woman and then he drove away in a silver sports car. It was the car that drew my attention; don't see many like that these days."

"Any idea who the woman was?"

"Nope, never seen her before or afterwards. Is there anything else as I am late? I promised to meet Brenda off the bus from work."

After getting the young man's address and identity number Jones let him go to meet the green bus they could see pulling in by the Post Office.

Jones and Smith agreed that Hughes was no longer a suspect but were very pleased that he had been able to identify Blount and his car as being in the vicinity.

"This is one piece of information that confirms your instinct about this place. A good start for tomorrow Jack."

Smith's day in Steyning started slowly. His plan was to visit some of the shops down the High Street, have coffee in the café and generally watch how the villagers spent their time. He wanted to find out more about both the Pope family and the Fletchers. He knew it was a long shot but the information from Newcastle that Blount had a stepsister down south 'in service' tweaked his interest. He knew that many big country houses still employed maids and housekeepers and the younger maids always like to boast about the goings on at their house. He was hoping that perhaps one of those young girls would let out information about an older servant with a northern accent. Smith knew the information he wanted would not come quickly he just had to ask the right questions and be patient. Finding the stepsister would be like looking for a needle in a haystack but that was true investigating, according to Smith's rule book.

After two cups of coffee and several meaningful side glances from the waitress Smith decided it was time to move on. His first call was at the butchers he didn't identify himself as a policeman, he just joined the long queue of housewives and waited patiently to be served. When it was his turn the man with the bloody apron and the straw hat asked.

"What can I get you?" Smith had promised Helen that he would pick up meat for dinner, so he ordered four juicy pork chops.

"You're lucky mate I've just got six left. No more until next week."

Smith was the last in the queue, so he asked the butcher if there were many big houses in the area that still had servants.

"Oh yes we deliver to several up at the end of the High Street and then out towards Ditchling, we even go as far out as Storrington. They all have maids and housekeepers still. Some even still have chauffeurs."

"Do you know if any have silver sports cars?"

"I'm not much good on cars. I know the Rolls Royce and the Jag and I have seen the young uns driving those fast cars around. The only one I know for sure is the red one that young Woolcott drives. The Woolcotts live just on the edge of town. But why don't you try Addison's down the road. He buys and sells cars and has been here for years. He was here before I came, and I've been here these twenty years."

It was young Mr. Addison that Smith spoke to.

"There's nobody in the village that owns a silver sports car like you're describing but I have seen one around. The driver always wears a cap and goggles so I can't describe him for you. But I do know he visits the pubs around as people have asked me who he is. I would start at the Shepherd and Dog at Poynings apparently that is one of his favourite pubs. Tell Bill that I sent you over."

It was almost opening time, so Smith drove over to Poynings just in time to see a group of hikers drop their gear outside the pub entrance and go in for their lunch. Smith ordered his usual half pint and sat at the back table watching the room. Soon the locals began arriving calling out their greetings and picking up their drinks as quickly as the barman could pour them. Smith could hear them as they argued about the London football teams, then they went on to the weather and then they began on local politics. Smith decided to step in before the conversation got really heated as he knew it surely would.

"Excuse me I'm a stranger around here," he explained, "but I was led to believe that somebody from this area had a silver sports car for sale."

"Well you're a bit old for a sports car aren't you?" laughed one of the younger men.

"Oh no it's not for me. It's for a friend; I said that as I was travelling through this area today, I would ask about the car."

"I don`t know anyone from here that owns a silver one, young Willie Woollcott owns a red one, but mostly it's sedans around here. "

"My friend was so sure it was from around here," said Smith, pulling on his coat preparing to leave.

"Just a minute," said another member of the group, "there is a bloke who comes around here sometimes who has a silver sports car. He lives in Brighton or Hove but he said he has business in Steyning and Ditchling so he stops off here for lunch."

"Do you know his name?"

"No. He was quite rude when Andrew here spoke to him, so we left him on his own, anti-social beggar that one. He used to sit at the back table, over there watching. Used to give us an uncomfortable feeling as if he was laughing at us. Maybe Bill would know more about him."

But Bill was as unfamiliar with the patron as the others. He recognized the description of both the man and the car but like the others said the visitor was very unsociable. Bill explained that he only came in about four times a month.

Smith was quite pleased with the information gathered on his first day and determined that the next day he would drive over to Ditchling, check out the church and ask more questions about the silver sports car over there. But now he had to get home as Tony, he and Helen's eldest son, was going through a difficult stage. Despite his parents' wishes Tony left school before he wrote his final exams and seemed to be without direction or motivation as he waited to be called up.

These post-war years were proving to be very difficult for many groups within the community. Unemployment hit various groups in different ways. Returning soldiers were actually lucky to find a job and even luckier if they were able to settle down into civvy life without much difficulty. Women were expected to give up their war time employment to the returning men and that didn't go down well especially as thousands of women were war widows with young families and needed every penny they could earn.

Conscription was still in force and boys of Tony's age wondered what to do for the two years until their papers arrived on their doorsteps. Helen and Jack wanted Tony to stay on until the sixth form and then go to college or university when he came out of the forces but like many others he thought school was a waste of time and he would rather get out and do something for two years. But what? Despite his parents' efforts to guide him to the employment exchange or to sign up for a government sponsored Apprenticeship program Tony seemed to be just wandering about with no firm ideas on how to use his two years and knowing what temptations were out there, his parents were very concerned about their son. Jack Smith was fully aware that despite the hardships of war and the country's very slow recovery, crime still marches on regardless.

The second call from Canada came through as expected and after exchanging pleasantries Inspector Pellam read out the report that Constable Waters had sent to him. It was a repeat of much that had been said over the telephone earlier but it did contain reference to a case where the wife of a candidate running for Parliament was accused of having an affair with a young man who worked on her husband's campaign. According to Waters he and Blount were assigned to deal with the complaint that had been laid by the young man's mother. They had both gone out to the woman's house in Patcham and read out the accusation but after a few questions Blount had sent Waters out of the house to wait in the car. Waters admitted that this was the usual routine for Blount especially when the case could have serious repercussions on the accused. Waters' report was very detailed and provided Jones with both the surname of the woman accused and the date he and Blount visited Patcham. His report also included the name of the doctor that Owen Steele had mentioned and the date of their visit to the clinic on Dyke Road.

At the finish of the report Jones thanked Pellam for his help and asked him to pass on their thanks to Waters.

"He did a fine job there, Inspector, and I must say by the look of it our loss is your gain as we lost a fine officer."

"I will do surely do that, "said Pellam in his western drawl," Always glad to help the folks back in the old country. Call anytime."

Jones chuckled as he put down the phone and decided that he would keep in touch with Inspector Pellam of the RCMP. "Life is certainly different out in Western Canada," he murmured to himself.

Checking the three active files against the details recalled by Waters it was obvious to Jones that at last he knew who two of the three remaining victims were.

As Smith was still away Jones had arranged to go up to Scotland Yard the following day to meet his friend Mac, a fellow Detective Inspector. They were currently working with other jurisdictions in the South to solve the ongoing hijacking of lorries carrying building supplies around the country. Everything in the country was still in short supply. Rationing was still on and petrol was still rationed. Consequently, instead of decreasing after the war ended black marketeering had increased tenfold and it seemed that every community had somebody who could wheel and deal for the right amount of cash.

There was a new breed of marketer seen around the busy shopping areas. Spivs, who in their turned-up collars, trilby hats and dark glasses trolled through local shopping areas dragging their handcart full of stolen goods to sell to the exhausted housewives who had money to spend but little to buy. The handcart was the spiv's specialty and when their mate would raise the alarm of an approaching policemen it was very easy to lift the handcart and dash off to hide down some nearby alley much to the shopper's amusement. But these traders were small fry, usually dealing in over ripe fruit and vegetables or small articles that came their way via another trader.

Mac had called to say that he had made some headway in the case of the murdered yachtsman found floating in Shoreham Harbour last year and he promised that by the time Jones reached the Yard he would have information on the whereabouts of young Donny Harrison.

While Jones and Smith were away from the office DC Masters was sent out to Rottingdean, to St. Dunstan's Hospital where returning service men who had any kind of eye injuries were treated. Masters had arranged a time to see Derek Bond to ask him about his time with Blount, but the young sailor was not interested in what Masters wanted.

As they sat together at a table in the cafeteria Masters couldn't help but stare at the slightly older man.

Bond was taller than Masters but had a stoop that made him seem both older and shorter than he really was. But it was his face that drew Masters' attention. He knew that Bond had lost his sight as a result of a bomb blast but Masters had not expected to see so much facial disfigurement. There was a deep purple scar running across Bond's face from one temple, across his nose and down past the end of his mouth into his neck. When Bond spoke although his words were natural his facial expressions bore little relation to the words coming out and his mouth hardly moved. His eyes were covered by dark glasses that did bobble up and down where the bridge of his nose should have been.

Masters was dismayed by his own fascination as he watched Bond's face. It was terrible to watch the effort the man made to communicate yet too fascinating to look away. Master's shook himself. Then he started to explain why he was there.

"This former Sgt Ray Blount was found murdered a couple of weeks ago and your Inspector up in Newcastle had told us that you were Blount's partner for a couple of years before you went into the navy."

"Yes, but that was a long time ago. Like another lifetime."

"Well my Inspector Jones was hoping that you might want to share with us anything that you think would help us solve his murder."

"You said that you had spoken to Sgt Scott. Well he tried to help me when I complained about Blount's behaviour but he, Scott, was always being put off by Crump. He was a good man, Scott, but Crump was just an idiot and to think I went to war so that people like Crump could be in charge!" Bond thumped his hand on the table.   Nervously Masters started again.

"If you could give us a few names of people who Blount dealt with that you think would be capable of killing him it would be a great help. Somebody like Donny Harrison for instance." Bond's angry reaction startled the constable.

"If you think I'm going to give you any help at all to catch that man's killer you are sadly mistaken. Donny's life was ruined because of Blount's lies. I'm glad that Blount is dead, that's the best bit of news I've heard for a long time."

Derek Bond struggled to his feet. "Now if you would kindly take me to the door, I have a treatment session to attend to try to get my life back together. Good morning Constable."

CHAPTER EIGHTEEN

Jones always enjoyed his visits to his friend Mac. Sometimes it was an official visit, as today, when it would be all business. That is until an hour before Jones' train was due to leave when they would saunter over to the pub outside Victoria station and get caught up on more personal happenings. Sometimes, on a Saturday, they met up outside Stamford Bridge to watch Chelsea play but as Mac had recently married those meetings were fewer. But now Mac had news for him.

"Remember that seaman you found floating in Shoreham harbour a year or so ago and you asked me to check into his activities and associates?" Jones nodded. "Well it seems he wasn't quite as snow white as his colleagues and friends thought. We knew his identity that evening, we knew that it was your missing yachtsman, but it seems he was a man of many identities. We sent his fingerprints through to Interpol and other European countries to find what he was really up to." Mac paused for breath. "In fact, he was a Swedish national and was one of the top members of a gang who organized the high jacking of consignments of wood and other profitable commodities. Not only here in Britain but on the continent as well, especially in France. Apparently, he controlled the activities until the goods were unloaded at our harbours and picked up by his men to be taken to the customer... He made arrangements with the managers of the wood mills to cut and load more wood than the invoice showed then he or a trusted gang member accompanied the goods across the channel to our ports on the South Coast where other gang members would take over the distribution of the wood. But according to an informer our friend had lately transferred his interest to diamonds and was building up his own web of diamond smugglers. He had many connections in Amsterdam and several over here. Mostly the diamonds would be exchanged for cash off-coast, out in the Channel and then, according to our source the stones would show up in markets anywhere. Since we discovered all this, we have been keeping an eye on the harbours, Shoreham especially, we know that the gang is still operating and if anything, they are getting bolder. By the increased activities around Hatton Garden we think there must be an influx of smuggled diamonds coming in."

"So, the wood is still being stolen and distributed mostly from the small harbours on the South Coast and the diamonds are also exchanged down here."

"'Fraid so Dai. But we do have some brighter news. We have two officers who have infiltrated the gang and are currently working up north. They have established concrete links between harbours; in some cases, harbour masters, and some crew members and also connections between some lorry owners and construction firms. Some of whom would appear on the surface to be legitimate, but now we know better."

"Any facts emerge to say why my man was killed at Shoreham?"

"Not yet but apart from a disagreement among thieves we'll have to wait until our people get further into the structure of the gangs that he was involved with."

"How much do our colleagues know about this progress?"

"I did let each of regional partners know and asked them to keep watch and report any new happenings to us. I don't want anybody stepping in prematurely as it could endanger our two men in there."

"Okay," said Jones, "that is good news. Any progress is good, but I'm still convinced that our old friend Mr. Moore, currently of Her Majesty's prison, Pentonville had a finger in this operation. And I wonder what our greyhound racing fraternity* will think of this news about their wealthy member."

"That should be an interesting meeting for you. No doubt we will dig up a link to Moore soon, but not yet. By the way your man Shady Lane was absolutely spot on with information about the body in Shoreham Harbour. Okay Dai time to go, I'm thirsty and I have news for you." Jones turned to his friend,

"Yes, what news?"

"It will keep for ten minutes besides I need a beer in my hand before I tell you. Come on." As Mac filed away his report Jones grabbed his raincoat and opened the door ready for a quick exit to the pub.

Dyke Road was a community of affluence, probably the most wealthy of all roads in Brighton or Hove. The houses were detached, individually designed and very large with the majority having enough land around them to have curved drives and multiple garages. Despite the wartime need for wrought iron these owners had managed to hang on to their tall black iron fences and many employed security staff at their entrance gates. One side of the road had Brighton addresses while the homeowners on the other side were citizens of the more sought-after address of Hove. The road stretched up to the crossroads leading to Devil's Dyke, a familiar place to Jones as he often walked across the top of the Downs from West Hove and down into Patcham. But neither he nor Smith had ever been inside one of these large houses.

The guard at the gate was not pleased to see them and churlishly asked if they had an appointment with Sir Michael as he wasn't allowed to let any stranger in unless they had an appointment and even then he had to call in and check it with Sir Michael's assistant. Jones produced his warrant guard and immediately the churlish man became an apologetic, whining figure, who at breakneck speed, was out of his hut opening the gates for Jones's car.

"Probably an old lag," chuckled Smith as he rang the doorbell. It was quickly opened by a dark suited young woman.

"Ah Ben said you were on your way. I am Miss Charmaine, Sir William's personal assistant. How can I help you gentleman?"

"We would like a few minutes of the doctor's time, we have a few questions to ask him, "explained Smith.

"May I ask what this is regarding?" asked Miss Charmaine, getting out her notebook.

"No may not ask," thundered Jones. "Tell the doctor we are here or take us to his office."

He was not about to bandy words with an assistant. The young woman was momentarily taken aback by Jones's tone of voice. She was the one who made appointments and looked after Sir Michael. She was not used to being ordered about. Gathering herself she indicated the two chairs and asked them to wait while she spoke to Sir William.

"I will give you two minutes and then we will come to find you," barked Jones.

Smith was also taken aback by Jones's attitude. He knew his Inspector to be a patient, empathetic person who treated people respectfully. He sat down quietly beside Jones and asked him if he was feeling alright.

"Yes Sgt. I am feeling fine, but you know we have been sorting out this case for more than two weeks now and I am fed up with running down blind alley always looking for clues. All we have done so far is to meet up with people who have committed a crime but have been willing to pay to cover it up rather than own up to what they did. Blount died a horrible death, but you know we had to dig out all his victims, not one came forward of their own account once they knew he was dead. Not even his stepsister to bury him. And now we are here with a man who has more money than we will ever see who has committed some crime or other and we have to consider him a victim. Look around I wonder how he suffered during the war!"

Just then a man in a morning suit opened the door and strode across to greet the officers.

"I am Sir Michael Crandall, and this is my clinic. How can I help you Inspector?"

"We are investigating the death of a former police officer Sgt. Ray Blount and it is our understanding that you have had dealing s with him."

"Ah shall we go into my office gentlemen. Miss Charmaine I will call you when I need you. This way please."

The three men walked through the entrance hall and into an office that was so lavishly furnished that it shouted wealth, prosperity and affluence from its four corners. Smith saw Jones' face and sensing Jones's growing annoyance, quickly asked.

"Are we correct in stating that you knew Sgt. Blount?"

"Yes, I knew the Sgt. He came to the clinic a few years ago to ask me some questions about a patient of mine."

"Can you remember what the matter was?" Jones's voice was sharp.

"Yes, I remember the visit very well because your Sgt was the rudest man I had ever met. It had been a terrible week here at the clinic we had lost a patient, a young woman, and we were all so sad that she hadn't survived the surgical procedure. It was after her funeral that her distraught brother went to the police station and laid a charge of negligence against me and my clinic. Sgt. Blount was investigating that accusation but after I had explained as much as I could without breaking doctor client privilege Sgt Blount left and I never heard a thing afterwards. Such a sad case."

"Did you ever meet the Sgt. after that incident?"

"No Inspector. Why would I have occasion to meet that man ever again!" The doctor's voice trailed off as he tried unsuccessfully to keep eye contact with Jones.

"Now if that is all I am a busy man and clients are waiting for my attention?"

"No, we are not finished Sir William. Please sit down again" ordered Jones. "A man like you must keep informed on local matters."

"Of course," agreed the doctor. "A man of my statue in the community must keep abreast of what is going on."

"Then you will be aware that former Sgt. Blount had left the police force several years ago and recently his body had been found in an empty house over in Steyning."

There was a pause as the man began to move some papers around on his desk. Keeping his eyes averted he finally spoke.

"Yes ahumm. I do seem to remember something about his being fired from the Force."

Jones leaned forward putting his elbow on the desk.

"And his murder? Is there any reason for us to think that you might be connected to his murder?" The doctor leaned back, away from Jones's penetrating eyes.

"No, no" he stuttered.

"Well we have proof that you did know Blount and that you were in touch with him as recently as earlier this month when you gave him his blackmail money. Why was he blackmailing you? What did he know that caused you to pay him for almost five years?"

The man reeled as he swayed back in his chair as if he had been struck. Then Jones came again.

"Did you get tired of paying him money and decided to get rid of him? Did you take him out to the empty house, kill him and then as a final gesture of contempt mutilate his body. As a surgeon you would know exactly where to cut and how to get rid of the blood? Is that what happened? Were you tired of being bullied around by some rotten copper?" Jones sat back in his chair, staring at Crandall until the silence simply forced the broken man to speak.

"Yes, I did pay Blount blackmail money. He would call and set up the meeting. Usually it was after dark and we would always meet somewhere along the seafront. By the Piers or outside the Grand Hotel. I hadn't broken the law, but he threatened to tell everybody that I had and said that he had proof. I would have been a ruined man. And yes, I had read about his murder in the paper. But I didn't kill him"

Smith interrupted. "I see that you have two beautiful children Sir William and I remember reading that your daughter was engaged to be married to a baronet, son of a Scottish Lord I believe. As a father with such good marriage prospects for your daughter Blount and his hold over you would be a real problem especially if Blount chose to speak out. You and your family would be finished. Is that not so Sir William?"

"Yes, yes all you say is right, but I didn't kill him. I don't even know the place where he was found. Errr…"

"What else have you to tell us?" coaxed Smith, "better you tell us here than at the station. What is it?" After a long silence the shaken man spoke.

"I did think about hiring somebody to get rid of Blount. I only wanted him frightened but when I read that he was dead I thought that the man I talked to had gone ahead before I had given him instructions. But I only wanted him frightened off, not killed."

Jones moved in quickly "What is this man's name and where does he live? Do you have a number for him?"

"His name is Richard Bennett. He was recommended to me by a colleague in London as somebody who might help me out. Bennett is a bouncer at a night club in Piccadilly. I called him at this number. I did meet with him a few weeks ago and I was frightened he was so big and strong certainly looked like a bouncer. I have tried his number several times since I read about the murder but couldn't reach Bennett. But I hadn't decided to go through with it, and I hadn't paid him, and he hasn't been in touch with me for any money, so I don't know if it was him or not." the doctor finished lamely.

"We will make enquiries with the Yard about your Richard Bennett and you will have to pray that he didn't act on your behalf. We'll be in touch" and with that Jones and then Smith quickly left the office. They passed Miss Charmaine in the corridor.

"Have you gentleman finished. Can I help you at all?"

Jones smiled grimly "I think it's your boss who needs the help, not us. Good day."

Outside Jones plunked himself down in the passenger seat. "You know Jack I feel much better after that little episode especially knowing that our pretentious surgeon friend is going to be sweating until we let him know about his Mr. Bennett."

Smith smiled; he was pleased that his Inspector had regained his humour. He too had experienced investigations that despite hard work the end result had not come easily or quickly.

"Now let's go back over the hill to Patcham and see what that lady has to say for herself," he said starting the car.

Mrs. Stewart was a lady in her late thirties. She was slim with honey blonde hair and was dressed stylishly in a blue silk dress and heeled shoes. After introductions were made, she invited the officers into her sitting room. The house was an original two-story home built soon after the village of Patcham became a dormitory for the people who travelled daily to their work in London. From the outside the house had the Elizabethan look complete with black beams and white plasterwork, but the inside was very modern.

The furniture was the latest in the Ercol style, light coloured wood, mostly oak; there was nothing ornate about the room just a smallish sofa, three armchairs, a narrow bookcase and some side tables. The mantelpiece was oak with a cream tiles surrounding the fireplace. On the mantelpiece were two pieces of Staffordshire china, two photographs of teenage boys and a stylish clock. A very comfortable room Smith thought.

Jones began the interview by explaining that he and Sgt. Smith were investigating the murder of Ray Blount.

"Did you happen to read about it a couple of weeks ago in the local paper?"

"Well yes I did. I keep an eye on what happens locally as my husband always wants to know what is happening in his constituency. My husband is the M.P. for this riding did you know?"

"Yes Mrs. Stewart we are well aware of who your husband is. Is he in London today?"

"Yes. He never misses a day when Parliament is in session."

"Mrs. Stewart we need to ask you some questions about your relationship with former Sgt. Blount. If you would rather wait until your husband can be with you, we can come back."

"I don't know why you think I would know this Sgt. Blount."

"We have it on good authority that during the month proceeding Election day in 1946 a complaint was laid against you by the mother of one of the young men who was on your husband's campaign team. Is that correct?" asked Jones.

Indignantly Mrs. Stewart asserted that she didn't know where the Inspector got his information from, but he was wrong. She strode across to the door and with as much dignity as she could muster, she asked them to leave her house. Neither of the men moved.

"Mrs. Stewart when Blount came out to see you that evening, he had with him another officer, a constable Waters who was asked to leave the room while you and Sgt. Blount had a private conversation. Constable Waters has testified that he knew what the complaint against you was and that he was indeed at this house that evening. Again, I offer you the opportunity to wait for your husband but believe me we will get to the bottom of your relationship with Blount."

The lady shut the door and walked over to the window staring out at the green of the Downs. She started to speak.

"It all began with the dam war. My husband was a quiet peace-loving man who enjoyed his gardening and his work equally. His family meant a great deal to him as did our quiet existence here in this small village community. But he came back a war hero with all the dash and bravado that all spitfire pilots seemed to inherit once they had those wings on their uniforms. I thought life would resume as before but within a few months of his demob he decided to run for Parliament and our life has never been the same since. It was during his campaign that I made the mistake of encouraging the attentions of a young man who regularly gave me a lift home when my husband was too busy to do so. I know I was wrong to encourage him, but I was so lonely and very angry that after spending almost all the war years at home looking after our two boys my husband didn't really want to spend time with me. Even now he is away more than he is home."

"What happened when Blount came to see you?"

"Your constable was right; he was ordered to wait outside while Blount put his blackmail proposal to me."

"Why did you agree to it?"

"What else could I do? My husband was going to win the election; my sons had a chance to attend better schools than here locally. If I had confessed everything would have come crashing down and although I would have had my husband home how long would he have stayed and how happy would we be. No Inspector I couldn't take that chance, so I agreed to Blount's terms."

Mrs. Stewart had remained very calm as she explained her situation and even seemed relieved that everything was out in the open.

"Where do I stand now Inspector?"

"You have done well confirming everything that we knew so far but we still have a couple of questions. First of all, where did you give the money to Blount? We know that your money was deposited by him regularly each month and that it was in cash, so you had to meet up with him somewhere. We need to know where."

"He would call me and set up the time and place. It was usually in the afternoon and would be somewhere out in the country. Sometimes a churchyard, sometimes a bench in a park, or walking around a local pond. Sometimes in Steyning, or Ditchling or even the smaller places in between. But never in town."

"Do you know these areas well?"

"Oh yes I often do my shopping in the country villages such a nice quiet atmosphere. I often meet a friend for lunch or coffee."

"Do you know the Baxter House at all?"

"Only that I have passed by it on several occasions when I`m shopping."

"Did you know that Blount`s body was found there?"

"Yes, I did," Mrs. Stewart smiled wryly "I must admit that I thought it was a wonderful place for a murder. Inspector, I wanted Blount out of my life, but I am not a murderess. The money I paid out to Blount is nothing compared to the future happiness of my boys."

"Well what do you think Sgt. have we met the murderer this afternoon?" asked Jones as they headed to their car.

"No I don`t believe so. Sir William is far too much of a physical coward to do this and Inspector no self-respecting hit man would do a job and not ask for the money, in fact they usually want the cash before the job is done. I think we`ll find that Mr. Bennett has absolutely nothing to do with this. As for Mrs. Stewart she didn`t appear to be bothered at all by Blount`s hold over her. She felt as long as she paid Blount her little world would be safe, although it is interesting that she is so familiar with the area around where the body was found."

"Okay let`s do a quick summary of where we are. Of the six active files we have met with five blackmail victims and the only ones that we could say are anyway near being suspects are; the doc. through his Mr. Bennett, Mrs. Stewart through her connection with both Blount and Steyning and her knowledge of Baxter House. I would rule out the actor, strong alibi, the shop owner, tough enough but not a killer, the headmaster but the dates don`t match up. We have one file left that is proving very difficult to trace and we still have not traced Blount`s long lost stepsister. Do we have anymore?"

"This is like a horse race sir we have so many in the race, but we can't predict the winner, so to speak. Oh, we still have young Mr. Hughes, but his alibi is perfect and then we have the ex-convict from Blount's Newcastle days, Donny Harrison. It will be interesting to see what Masters got from that fellow at St. Dunstan's."

"Any ideas on where to go next?"

"Yes, I have been thinking about the next step. We know that Blount knew his way around the Steyning area, his car was seen by several local citizens and he often stopped at the Shepherd and Dog. I think the neighbours close to the Baxter House need to be looked at a little closer. Let`s concentrate on the House and the people who had any connection at all with it. We don`t know much about the Pope's or the

Fletcher's so let's go back to Mr. Siddely and see if he has remembered anything and then to the neighbours."

"Sounds good to me, and let's add the former housekeeper to that list. We'll go tomorrow, I need a trip into the country again. In the meantime, I will call Mac at the Yard and see if he has anything on Mr. Richard Bennett. And I will send young Masters and Atkinson up to Somerset House to see if they can track down Blount's stepsister. They need some practice in the use of marriage and birth certificate tracing."

"Yes" said Smith, chuckling at the vision of the young officers ploughing through the heavy tomes of certificates. "Will you let Masters drive them up to London? He has a new car and I know he's itching to try it out on the London to Brighton Road. I'll get Masters now and then let Sgt. Hewitt know that we will be on his patch tomorrow. Shall I ask him to meet us at Baxter House and we can start from there?"

"Yes, it will be good to have him along with us. How about saying 10-00 in the morning? I'd like to leave here a little earlier as I want to pop into Trent's office. Just a short visit." Jones avoided Smith's glance and looking at his notes asked Smith to get Masters.

The young constable did not have much to report regarding the case only that Bond had refused to tell him anything about Donny Harrison.

"It would seem that Bond feels that Blount deliberately stitched up Harrison and ruined his life."

"Does he know where Harrison is now?"

"He refused to tell me anything Sir, only that Blount's murder was the best bit of news he had heard for a long time."

"Not very helpful," muttered Jones.

"Yes sir, but you should see him Inspector. His face is a mess, he doesn't have any nose at all, and he is blind. You can't really blame him for being so bitter," blurted out Masters.

Jones and Smith looked at their young colleague, not knowing quite what to say.

"Once this case is over would it be alright if I went to see him? His parents are very elderly and cannot get down from Newcastle very often. He says he has nobody down here at all. I could go and read to him or take him out along the cliff for a walk." The young constable's voice just trailed off.

"Yes of course. He is not involved in the investigation as a suspect so go ahead. I'm sure the young man would appreciate some young company."

"Early night Sir?" asked Smith.

"I'm going to walk up to The Castle and hopefully run across Shady Lane. Who knows it might be my lucky day and he has heard of some scouces who have been visiting Sussex lately and could just possibly have known Blount."

As usual Shady was holding up the bar with a half full glass in his hand and as usual Shady was dressed to the nines. Jones nodded to him and worked his way through the crowd of drinkers.

"Evening Mr. Jones," said Shady. He preferred not to refer to the Inspector by rank, it was not always the best thing to be seen drinking with the local bobby.

"Evening Shady. Looking sharp tonight, new outfit?"

"Oh, I went up to Petticoat Lane a couple of weekends ago. Got them all for a fiver."

He lovingly smoothed down the crease of his black and white checkered trousers then pulled at the cuffs of his jacket which was also black and white check but of a different shade and size check. Finally, he fingered his white shirt and black bow tie.

"Gotta keep up with the fashions. That's what me mum always said," he said grinning at the policeman as he took a gulp of his beer. "So you 'aven't come to admire my clobber, what do you want to know?"

"As you know we are still looking into the death of Blount and now we know that he spent some time with the Newcastle force before he ended up down here. I was hoping that perhaps you had some contacts from up there who could help us out. You see it turns out that Blount had a stepsister, a little older than him, but nobody seems to know her name or where she ended up," explained Jones.

"Strange that," said Shady. "I wus up at the racetrack a week or so ago and ran into a couple stable hands from up north. We got talking and they asked me about the murder of the policeman. But they had no idea he was actually from their part of the country, or even that he was on the Force up there. Apparently, he did like to go to the races, and they knew him from several of the tracks up there."

"Did they know him personally`

"No and they didn`t want to by all accounts. He had a reputation of bullying the bookies and had even beaten one up when he thought he was being cheated. They stayed clear of him," Shady grinned into his beer.

"I know that look," said Jones. "What else do you know that I should know?"

"Another beer here please," Jones called to the barman. "Here drink this and tell me what you know."

After taking a couple of swallows Shady wiped his mouth saying. "I know that Blount had a girlfriend after his wife left him. And I know who she was and where she lives!"

"That is a surprise. The first time we have heard about a woman with Blount. Now you have finished your beer I want to know all you know about this lady."

"Well she aint no lady I can tell you that," smirked Shady, "her name is Peggy Makins and you can always find her at the Great Globe up St. James's St."

Sliding off the barstool Jones put cash on the bar, "Here you've earned another on me," and left the pub. He retraced his steps to his office and left a message for Masters to track down all information on a Peggy Makins who could usually be found at the Great Globe. Masters was to report to Jones as soon as he had information.

CHAPTER NINETEEN

Sgt. Hewitt met them outside Baxter House. Jones wanted to concentrate on the neighbours who could actually see Baxter House either through their windows or across the fields. His aim was to find out the routine of each of the former occupants of Baxter House as well as any unusual things that neighbours often see but don't remember until their memories are jogged. Sgt. Hewitt had drawn a rough map showing the location of four houses that he felt would fit Jones's need.

"We'll go together," suggested Jones. "But at each one I want you both to take turns going around the outside in case there is something we have missed."

The owners of the first house were an elderly retired couple. He had taught in a school in Croydon and she was a primary teacher at the local school. They had been fully retired for five years now but had lived in the house for over thirty years. Sgt. Hewitt introduced Jones to Mr. and Mrs. Nash

"Yes, we knew the Pope's quite well. They were older than us of course and had lived here much longer than us. He used to run a small holding on his land and Mrs. Pope was like Marie, a primary teacher, but at a school over in Ditchling."

"Can you tell us anything about their family?"

"The Pope's didn't have any children and as far as we could see they had very few visitors to their house especially once they retired. They had Miss Rowington who looked after them and I heard that they became very dependent on her as they aged. Mr. Pope did have a car when he was working but he had to give it up. Although he still drove his old tractor around the country roads sometimes. I asked him about that, and he said that he just liked to have a run out now and then. He would go across and watch the animals or go down to the stream to fish."

Jones moved across to their window.

"I notice that you can see the Baxter House from here. As I explained we are investigating the murder of a former colleague whose body was found in that house and to help us in our investigation I would

like both of you to think for a few minutes to see if you can remember anything strange or unusual that happened around that house."
Mrs. Nash spoke out. "We did report seeing young Stuart Hughes back this spring. He was out the back looking around."

"Yes. We have interviewed Mr. Hughes and he has a strong alibi for the time we think the murder took place."

"I said earlier that the Pope's didn't have many visitors," recalled Mr. Nash "but after his wife died and he was on his own we did see a strange car at the house. Not very often, about every couple of months or so. We knew it wasn't the doctor or Mr. Siddely his solicitor, as we know their cars We did pop in to see the old chap when he was on his own, just to be neighbourly, but he had no idea who the car belonged to and told me I must be seeing things, he said he had never seen or heard a car. I didn't press him as by then he was becoming quite confused."

"Thank you very much for your help. If you remember anything else that could help us please call my number," said Jones as he handed them his card.

Sgt. Hewitt had been walking around outside the Nash's house testing the sight lines down to the Baxter House but had nothing unusual to report. The next house the officers visited was to the back of the Baxter House. Their knock was answered by a young woman holding an infant in her arms.

"Mrs. Brown?" asked Smith.

"Yes, can I help you?" was her friendly greeting. Jones introduced himself and the two Sgts. and explained that they were making inquiries about the former owners of the Baxter house.

. 	"Come in come in. Don't leave the door open or my Billy will run out and somebody will have to catch him."

Just then a red headed boy, about four years old, came screaming around the corner into the hallway with his arms outstretched pretending to be an airplane.

"Billy, I need you to be quiet for a little while. Go and play with your bricks that daddy made you." `Billy sat himself in a corner with his bricks and the woman, still holding the baby, sat on the sofa.

"Ì didn`t know the owners of that house. I only met the Fletchers when my husband and I moved here when he came out of the army and they were soon gone to Australia. Mind you he would know them as he lived with his parents in that farm at the bottom of the lane. They've been here years. You'd best ask them. This house was empty for a few years before we moved in. My husband's parents own both this one and theirs and they were keeping this one for their daughter to live in, but she went off and married some Canadian soldier and moved over there. That caused an upset in the family I can tell you. But I don't think I can help you. Go down the road and speak to Harry's folks that'll do you more good."

Jones and Hewitt thanked Mrs. Brown for her help and then let themselves out of the door remembering to keep an eye out for young Billy. Smith reported that there was little to see outside with the only view of the Baxter House being the top of the upper floor and the roof and its chimneys.

"Well now let's visit with the Browns, Browns senior that is," said Jones.

The older Browns were not really old, somewhere in their mid-fifties, judged Smith. By the large herd of milking cows in the nearby fields they seemed to be successful farmers. At first it seemed that they had nothing to add to the information supplied by the Nashs but were able to confirm that they too had seen a strange car parked outside.

"It only started coming around just after Betty died, that is Mrs. Pope. We were great friends and it was a shock when she died so suddenly. I couldn't believe it when the postman told me what had happened."

"What did happen Mrs. Brown?"

"Well she fell down the stairs like. One minute she was at the top and the next minute she was at the bottom with 'er neck broken. Just like that. We couldn't believe it could we Will? We saw a police car out there the next day, but the doc. had reported it and they 'ad a inquest but it was said to be accidental. They said she must have tripped over a loose mat or something at the top of the stairs. Mr. Pope wasn't long after Betty, he couldn't live by himself. The housekeeper was very good and kind to 'im but he did miss his Betty so. We did see that strange car after Mr. Pope was taken into hospital but not as often. He never did come back. I really miss them we were good friends."

"What happened to the housekeeper, do you know?" Mr. Brown answered.

"Yes, Pope left her a house somewhere near Ditchling and as far as I know she still lives there."

"Did you know her well?"

"No. not really. She was from up north somewhere. Betty told my wife that she had come down years before and had a job as a nurse in Portsmouth or somewhere like that but had retired and had answered the Pope`s ad for a housekeeper. She`d been with them a few years, probably about ten as far as I can remember."

"The Pope`s never had any children, did they?"

"No Betty was always upset about that and made a great fuss over her niece. I haven`t seen her for a long time," Mrs. Brown explained.

After knocking unsuccessfully several times at the fourth house on their list they had a quick look around the back of the house and were preparing to leave when Hewitt, who had ventured further down the sloping garden, suddenly called out.

"Inspector you'd better come and have a look at this." Hidden under a pile of branches in the gully formed by a dried creek they could just see the outline of a car's headlight. As they pulled away the branches a small black sedan car was revealed. Although the wheels and all the seats had been removed its shiny paintwork showed that the car had not sat long in its hiding place. The road license disc had been scratched off and both the front and back plates were missing.

"We were wondering how Blount was transported to Baxter House when both his cars were still in Hove, perhaps this is the car the killer used. It isn't too far from the Baxter House. Perhaps they used this one for the killing and had another car waiting," said Jones.

"Or, if the killer was local, they could have walked home or picked up a bus. Both the Nashs and the Browns told us that the mystery car they saw was either green or silver but this one is black, so this wasn't that car. We will have to get the garage to tow this car in. Whether it belongs to this case or not it certainly looks as though somebody had reason to keep it well hidden."

Masters and Atkinson had been anxiously waiting for Jones and Smith to return to the station as they had good news for the Inspector. Masters started on his report.

"We started as you said Sir by checking out Ray Blount's birth certificate that gave us a starting date and his father's name for the other details. We found the marriage certificate between his father and a Cynthia Rowington, that was dated 1901. Then we back tracked the Rowington woman and found a birth certificate for a daughter named Elizabeth dated, 1894. Is that helpful Inspector?" finished Masters

"Yes. It certainly is because now we have proof that Blount's stepsister was called Elizabeth Rowington. There are many short forms for Elizabeth one of which is Bertha, which leads us straight to the Pope's housekeeper, Bertha Worthington. At last we have a concrete connection."

"But sir," said the calm voice of Sgt. Smith. "The housekeeper we met claimed not to know Blount. Claimed not to have a driving license and is a fragile, bird-like little old lady who wouldn't seem to have the strength to have done all that to Blount's body."

"Well maybe she is not the killer but that so called fragile old lady knows much more than she is telling us and we need to pay her another visit. Good work Constables you have found me something I can work on," finished Jones.

When the constables had left the office and Smith had gone to check with the garage about towing the hidden car in, Jones settled down to summarize what they had learned about the housekeeper. Bertha Rowington was Blount's bullying stepsister, although she never stepped forward to claim his body. Her employer, Mrs. Pope, died mysteriously although the housekeeper never came under suspicion. The housekeeper had formerly been a nurse. And now lived in a house bequeathed to her by the late Mr. Pope. Jones slapped his pen down frustration.

"Nothing of which makes her our murderer"

Just then Smith came in. "I bought you that one file we couldn't decode but with what the boys bought in I think we have it solved. Look sir the initials match with the housekeeper's and the date of the case is very close to the time of Mrs. Pope's death. Actually, I got Dr. Marshall to check his records and the death was two days before this date," he said pointing to the tab on the file, "and the inquest was two weeks later. So it would all fit."

"You're saying that it's likely that Blount was actually blackmailing his own stepsister on suspicion of murdering her employer. What a bastard that man was!"

"The other thing is that the mystery car that neighbours saw at the Baxter House after Mrs. Pope's death could have been Blount's. It all fits."

"Yes, you're right but I still have difficulty in visualizing that frail woman as being able to manhandle Blount's body about and do what was done to his corpse."

"Don't forget sir we are still living in an upside-down world. Women worked in shipyards and munitions factories. They helped build tanks and planes, they drove big heavy lorries. They moved supplies about the country and did all that we expected a man to do during the war so we shouldn't be surprised if a frail, little thing like the housekeeper actually had the strength to murder Blount."

"What about motive? After paying Blount for those years what suddenly prompted her to put an end to the blackmail arrangement by killing Blount off?"

"I don't know sir," answered Smith. "But my feeling is that we are almost there. Perhaps we need to take another visit out to see Miss Rowington?'

Jones looked up at Smith, "When this case is solved it will be your triumph. You had the instinct to keep going back to Steyning and it paid off. I have much to learn from you Jack and I want you to know how much I appreciate working together. I hope we can do that for several years to come."

Smith was embarrassed by his superior's praise and gently reminded Jones that they hadn't wrapped up the case yet.

"Where to next?" was Smith's only comment?"

"I am going along to the Super's office show him what we have and get him to get us a warrant for the housekeeper's house. We should be able to go out there in the morning. Will you get WPC Jenkins to come and both Masters and Atkinson. Oh, and call Sgt. Hewitt I'm sure he would like to be in at the kill. Smith looked at his boss, "Sorry Sgt. bad choice of words."

CHAPTER TWENTY

The three police cars sped along the country road before all the morning mist had burned off. There was little conversation in any of the cars. Each officer had been given their duties and knew exactly what to do once entry was gained into the house. Miss Rowington had not been warned of their visit although they knew that she was an early riser and expected that she would be able to see them coming over the brow of the hill down into her small community. Sgt. Hewitt and Constable Pearce were parked at the other end of the village and would see the three cars as they breasted the hill.

Politely but firmly Jones knocked on the door and quickly turned the door handle striding straight into the small living room.

"What on earth is the matter? Why have you come into my home without my permission?" demanded the frail voice. Smith and Jones held up their warrant cards for her to see and then handed her the search warrant issued by the local magistrate.

"Sit down Miss Rowington we have some more questions for you to answer?" She curled herself up on the armchair and pouting said that she had already told them everything she knew about Baxter House.

"We are more interested to know of your relationship with the policeman whose body we found in the house."

"I don't know what you mean Inspector. I didn't know the officer at all," she whined as she started to fiddle with the cuffs of her sleeve. "And what are those men doing with my things in my bedroom?"

"We have permission to search your house as we do not believe you are telling us everything," stated Jones. "Tell us about your former employer the late Mrs. Pope."

"Oh, she was such a sweet lady, very kind to me. She and her husband gave me this house to live in."

"How did she die?"

The whining voice continued. "Oh, she slipped on a mat at the top of the stairs. So sad it was, I was always telling her not to go down the stairs by herself, but she could be so stubborn and down she went. I was in the kitchen at the time and just heard the bump as she hit the bottom."

"The police came out to investigate. Do you remember the name of the officer who came to ask you questions?"

"No, you can't expect me to remember that far back. I'm an old lady myself my memory isn't so good."

She was still fiddling with her sleeves and refused to look at either officer.

"Miss Rowington it has come to our attention that soon after Mrs. Pope died you began to have a fairly regular visitor who would leave their car parked at the side of the house."

"Oh, that would be the doctor or Mr. Siddely the solicitor, they often came out to see Mr. Pope." She got out of her chair and made as if to see them out of the front door.

"No Miss Rowington we have not finished yet, please sit down; we are going to be here a while yet."

Jones looked across at Smith, they both knew that unless the constables found something incriminating soon, they would have to resort to bluffing to try to get to the truth. Jones pulled a manila envelope out of his pocket and sat tapping the envelope on his knee. "You say that you never knew Sgt. Blount but I put it to you that Sgt. Blount was the officer who came to investigate Mrs. Pope's accident and during his investigation he realized that you were his step sister whom he had last seen thirty years ago. I also put it to you that he was blackmailing you regarding the so-called accidental death of Mrs. Pope and that he was the visitor who periodically came to visit you at Baxter House and parked his car in the drive there."

"No." she shouted at Jones. The small frail lady had finally found her voice. "That is not true. I have never met that man before."

"But in this envelope we have the marriage certificate showing that Ray Blount's father married your mother in 1901. We also have your birth certificate showing your mother's name as Cynthia Rowington and your father's name as Barry Rowington. What happened to your father?"

"Oh, he died in the Boer war." When she realized how she had been caught she flew into a rage and tried to strike Jones. Smith intercepted but had difficulty in stopping the raging woman. It took both him and the WPC to wrestle the small woman back into her chair."

"Are you ready to start again Miss Rowington?" asked Jones after a few minutes. She was silent and seemed miles away.

"I've noticed that you have only one photo on your mantelpiece. Who is the little girl with you?" She looked sharply at Jones.

"That is the Pope's niece, the one who went to Canada. She and I did well together, and it reminds me of happier times."

"Was Blount blackmailing you in regard to Mrs. Pope's accidental death? I want the truth Miss Rowington?"

She straightened her narrow shoulders as she regained her defiant tone. "Yes, that little bastard was taking money from me every month. He said he could prove I pushed her down the stairs, but I didn't, she slipped on the mat. Besides there were others who were giving him money. Why don't you go and knock on their door?"

"Oh, I think we have found them all now, but you know Miss Rowington you are the one we can't quite figure. You knew Blount, he was blackmailing you, you knew the Baxter house and you must have known about the secret tunnel. So, everything points to you. Why did you kill him? Was it because you grew tired of paying out the money? Did he threaten to tell all to the police?"

She smiled ruefully at him, "Obviously Inspector you didn't know Ray very well. He hated the police, all he wanted was the means to get dirt on people so that he could squeeze them dry and his police uniform gave him the authority to get information and the power to use it for his own ends. He would never have spilt the beans about his little scheme. Oh no not Ray Blount. Somebody had to kill him before he would stop."

"Did you kill him Miss Rowington?"

She just started out of her window. There was a light knock on the door and Masters put his head around seeking permission to enter. He was holding two scrapbooks in his arms.

"I think you had better take a look at these, sir. I found them in a drawer under a sofa in the back room."

Jones flipped through the books and then stopped, staring at the open page then he flipped some more pages. Finally, he strode across to the housekeeper.

"Miss Rowington I am going to ask you for the last time did you kill Ray Blount and place his remains in Baxter House? It would serve you well to tell us now before we drag you down to the station. We know about Blount's blackmail scheme and we know what kind of man he was. He was certainly no credit to the police force. If you tell us what happened, it could be easier for you when it comes to your sentence."

The small sitting room was filled with tension as the silence grew.

"Will my daughter have to know?" she asked, without turning her eyes from the window.

"I assume that you are referring to the girl and then this young woman in these scrapbooks?"   She nodded. Jones continued.

"We know this lady as Mrs. Stewart who is the wife of Mr. Ian Stewart M.P is she your daughter?"

"Yes." Jones moved across the room so that he could look at the lady whose eyes remained firmly on her garden.

"Mrs. Steward will have to be told. But if you tell us what happened we will do all we can to keep your relationship out of the newspaper."

Bertha Rowington began to rock as she continued to look over her garden.   "Recently my daughter had been told that her husband was being considered for a seat on the Cabinet. I remember that day very well. Although we had agreed to keep our relationship a secret, we often met for lunch pretending that she was a niece of a friend of mine. On this day I could see she was desperate with worry. At first she wouldn't tell me why she was so worried but gradually she told me about her foolish affair with that young man and that she was being blackmailed by Blount." The rocking continued. "I could hardly believe it that she was being blackmailed by the same man who was taking my money. What a dreadful coincidence. A man who took money off his own stepsister and now his step niece- although he didn't know that at the time. It was then that I knew something had to be done. I knew that there were still others who were Ray's victims and I thought that if I did it nobody would suspect a frail old woman like me.   It wasn't for me, but I needed to protect my daughter and her two boys. It made me incredibly angry that by chance the future happiness of my daughter and my grandsons were in the hands of a man who I thought was out of my life forever." She turned her head towards Jones, "You don't really have any idea who murdered Ray do you? And now you have found the scrapbook you think your case is all sewn up. Well it isn't because as much as I planned and wished him dead, I did not do it."

"It doesn't look very good for you Miss Rowington. We have been able to connect you to both Blount and Baxter House. We know you have nursing experience and we know that Blount was blackmailing you. We had all we needed except the motive and now your scrapbook and your daughter's involvement have given us the motive. "

"Ah yes a mother's pride. But I did not kill him," was the defiant response.

CHAPTER TWENTY-ONE

It was early evening Smith and Jones were seated at the bar in the King and Queen.

"Do you have any doubts at all that we have Blount's killer?" asked Smith as he lifted his glass of beer.

"Well, everything fits. We have proven motive and means but you know, if we had a confession I would feel much more secure in charging her," replied Jones. "Like some of the other blackmail victims she had reached the end of her tether and was planning to do something to get rid of Blount but she insists that she never completed those plans and so far we haven't been able to break her. I have never come across a case with so many victims. And where the victimizer ultimately becomes the chief victim. But it's also been a very sad case because Bertha Rowington took action to prevent her own daughter from Blount's vicious nature regardless of the danger to herself." Jones added "Her daughter was in this evening and insists that despite our evidence her mother would never have committed such a crime. The biggest problem is that we have no definitive time of death for Blount. The nearest we have is a span of a week.

"Are you going to charge her?" asked Smith.

"We only have a few hours to make up our minds and now that her son-in-law has sent in his solicitor for her we are under the gun. I think that I'll go back to the station and have a chat with the Super, lay out what we have and see what his thoughts are,"

"Yes, I heard he was working late. I'll come in with you."

The silence in the room was heavy as each of the three men stared at the writing on the board. The Super finally spoke. "I guess we will have to go back and revisit any of the blackmail victims who could possibly have been in that vicinity during that week. Who do you have Sgt.?"

Smith walked across to the board, "Possibly the doctor's hit man, possibly young Hughes. The actor Davies is clear. Mr. Palmer was dead before the murder we think. Mrs. Ainslee`-well maybe, she's one tough lady but I believed her when she said she would not swing for Blount."

"But," said Jones moving to the board. "The only ones on that list who have a connection to Baxter House are Hughes and Rowington. Hughes was on base for six weeks which covered the time of death, so we are left with the housekeeper."

Smith spoke up. "What about Blount's girlfriend Peggy Makins; anything there?"

Jones answered, "It seems that she left him a couple of years earlier. She told Masters that Blount was much too rough for her and she didn't like his mates. So, she told him to shove off and leave her alone. Which apparently, he did, and they never met again."

Smith stood scratching at his chin. Jones moved his finger across the board re-checking the names. The Super suddenly stood up, crossed over to the board and pointed at Walker's name.

"Why is his name here?"

"He and Miss Wilcox found the body."

"Why was Walker there?"

Smith and Jones answered together, "He was looking at the house to buy. Damn," exploded Jones. "I missed that. Jack call Trent, at home if necessary, and see who else has viewed Baxter House since it has been up for sale."

It was a long half an hour before Mr. Trent called through. "Sorry to be so long but I had to drive back to the office. As we said before not many have been through Baxter house and the only viewer who wasn't local were a couple by the name of Palmer. They were looking for a place to enjoy retirement and he wanted to start a tree nursery. I believe he was a teacher and wanted something entirely away from education. Is that helpful Inspector?"

"Yes, indeed it is. Thank you so much." Jones turned to the others. "Well, well what a surprise. The Palmers went to view Baxter House a few months ago, looking for a place to buy for their retirement. He wanted acreage to start a tree farm. Obviously, our lady of the manor is not above telling a few lies. I wonder what else she is holding back."

"Are we going back there tonight?" asked Smith.

"No. The gates will be locked and if you remember Greenslade said once they are closed, they remain closed until 7 am the next morning. Which also means that Mrs. Palmer cannot leave? Jack, get hold of Masters and Atkinson and have them drive out to the school to watch the grounds just in case Mrs. Palmer has another way to leave. Tell them to call in if they spot any movement around the Palmer house. Don't let her leave the grounds and we will be out as soon as we can in the morning. She has a black Morris, but she might borrow a car from a friend so tell them to be watchful."

Smith left to find Masters and Atkinson who were waiting in the canteen for instructions.

"What will you do now Dai?" asked Young.

"First of all, I'm leaving urgent instructions for Jenkins to find out all she can about the Palmers. Especially Mrs. Palmer I need to know her background, who she was before she was married. Family connections. Jenkins is in about 7.30am so she can get onto that early. There's not much I can do at this time of night but first thing tomorrow Jack and I will take a run out to the Nash's place in Steyning. They are the closest neighbours to the Baxter House and if I remember correctly, they were both teachers, perhaps there is a connection there that would be useful."

By eight o'clock the next morning Jones and Smith were on their way to Steyning to visit the Nashs. Masters had reported that as far as he could tell Mrs. Palmer had not left her house. The maid had arrived about 8 o`clock and Mrs. Palmer had let her in. WPC Jenkins had made some progress on researching the Palmer family, learning that Mr. Palmer had come from an academic family in Shropshire but that he was an only child with both parents now deceased. Jenkins was now working on Mrs. Palmer's family.

Smith tapped his hand on the steering wheel. "You know Sir I was thinking just how strange this case was. I mean we had one of our own murdered and laid about so in Baxter House. Then we had a pile of suspects each of whom had reason to see our man dead. We find a missing sister who becomes our main suspect and now we're looking at a woman who nobody had even given a second thought to."

"And we've travelled, in a manner of speaking, from Brighton all around Sussex countryside, to Newcastle, to Canada, to Australia and now back to Steyning and as you say we have two suspects, both women. Who would have thought that?" commented the Inspector.

"Well here we are let's hope the Nashs are home this morning," said Smith as he parked the car outside the cottage. But he'd not have worried as Mr. Nash was already opening the door.

"I saw you pull in and wondered if there was anything wrong?"

"No Sir, I just need to ask a few more questions and then I think we can wrap up our investigation. May we come in?"

"Yes of course Marie is out the back I will call her in. Please sit down I'll just be a moment."

"Good morning Inspector, Sergeant, "said Mrs. Nash as she folded away her apron.

"Good morning. We are sorry to intrude on your day, but we have received some important information regarding the murder of the policeman, and we think you are the best people to help us just now... "

"Anything we can do to help," answered Mr. Nash

"First of all, you were both teachers; is that correct?"

"Yes," Mr. Nash answered.

"In your professional life did you ever meet a Mr. William Palmer who taught at The Grange the boy's school?"

"Yes, I knew him from various meeting we attended together. But my wife only knew him from the time I invited William and his wife over for tea when I knew he was looking over Baxter House. He had shared with me his hopes of starting a tree farm for his retirement and he asked me what I knew about Baxter House, so I invited the both of them to come over after they had seen the place."

"What did you think of the Palmer's? I would like an honest opinion. Mrs. Nash how did the Palmer's strike you?"

"I though Mr. Palmer seemed to be under a tremendous stress. His hands shook when he held the teacup and he seemed so indecisive when we asked him what he thought of the house."

"That's right;" continued her husband. "He was almost a different man than the one I met professionally. I asked him about the house and explained what I knew. I had explored the fields and outhouses many times as a boy, so I told him how the creek flooded in spring and how some of the lower meadow stayed spongy damp for several weeks after that. I also told him about the tunnel that connected the greenhouse to the main house and was used to keep the vegetables dry and cool in the winter."

"And Mrs. Palmer was here during that conversation?"

"Oh yes she was sat right there in that chair although she didn't seem very interested in our conversation. Did she Marie?"

"No, actually I took an instant dislike to her. She was so aloof from the conversation and seemed to be looking down her nose at our home. Don't want to speak ill of the dead but I'm very relieved that they will not be taking Baxter House."

"The last question, do either of you know anything at all about Mrs. Palmer's family background?"

"I know that William's father was headmaster at a college in Shropshire and that his mother was very busy socially. But that's all."

' "And Mrs. Palmer?"

"No, we didn't know anything about her other than she had some friends in the village that she had tea with sometimes. But I didn't know any of them," Mrs. Nash said.

"This gets more interesting by the minute. What do you think Jack?" as they walked across to the car.

"That couple in there have no idea how important their information is to our case. What a piece of luck that both men were teachers. What now" asked Smith as he started the car? "Where are we going?"

"Jack we are going over to visit the headmaster's widow. But before we leave here call in and tell the Superintendent we are going and ask him to join us. Oh, ask him to bring Policewoman Jenkins with him we'd better have a woman with us this time. I take it Masters and Atkinson are still there?"

"Oh yes and they will be looking forward to a few hours rest no doubt"

"Good then we have enough people. Let's go Jack. Finally, we have a solid connection. Although it does look as though I owe Bertha Rowington a very large apology."

CHAPTER TWENTY-TWO

Mrs. Palmer was annoyed at their presence back in her house. Although she was somewhat mollified to have the superintendent present.

"Supt. Young I am glad at least to see someone in authority visit with me but I have no idea why the Inspector feels he needs to visit me once again, unless it's more information about my husband's death. But that is surprising as I thought everything had been settled and I am almost ready to leave this place."

"We just have a few more questions Mrs. Palmer. Do you ever drive into Steyning?"

"Yes often, at least once a week. I like to shop there and sometimes I meet a couple of friends for afternoon tea. It's a pleasant drive across the Downs."

"I just want to confirm that it is correct that on our last visit here you said that you knew nothing about your husband's connection with the man whose body was found in Baxter House."

"That's right. I didn't know. I don't even remember his name. Bailey was it or something like that?" she said impatiently

"Mrs. Palmer did you know that Baxter House is currently up for sale. Did you ever visit Baxter House?"

"My husband made arrangements to see several houses. He was looking for a change and wanted to move away from the grounds here. But I can't remember all the places we went to and we didn't go forward with any purchase. Is that all Inspector? I am tired and I would like to be left alone now."

"You have nothing else to tell us?"

"What would I have to tell you? I know nothing. You told me about the blackmail and that horrible man. I knew nothing before that." Just then the maid entered the room. "I'm sorry madam but the Inspector is wanted outside."

Jones left the room; he knew that Jenkins had been waiting outside in the car for a final confirmation of some new information.

"Here it is Sir, just come through." She handed him a note.

"Fine, this is just what I needed, it's really good news. Come in with me."

"Sorry about the interruption" Jones said as he re-entered the room. "Now, where were we?"

"You are here, in my living room and delaying my packing. Now do you have any more questions, Inspector? Superintendent as you have taken up enough of my time?"

"One or two more and then we will be done," said Jones.

"Mrs. Palmer are you the daughter of Mr. Albert Willis, late of Guilford, who was a veterinarian."

"Yes. What is this about? My father has been dead a year now?"

"We are aware of when your father died but the estate has still to be settled as there were many debts to be sorted out. Is that correct?"

"Yes."

"And you still have access to his clinic which is as he left it when he died, with all his instruments, medicines, including poisons sitting on the shelves."

"Yes, but they are kept in a locked cupboard," she answered defiantly.

"But who has the key to that cupboard full of poisons? Not the solicitor my office has just checked. He says that you have the key. Is that correct?"

"Yes. But I have lost it. I don't remember when, but it is gone."

The officers stood up.

"Mrs. Palmer," said Jones, "I'm arresting you in regards to the murder of former police sergeant Ray Blount. Sergeant please ask the maid to bring in Mrs. Palmer's things as we are leaving for the station now."

Mrs. Palmer was struggling as WPC. Jenkins tried to assist her to get up out of the chair, "Take your hands off me. How dare you treat me like this? I will not say a word until my solicitor is here."

"That's fine Mrs. Palmer. We will call him, and he will meet us at the station. Now stand up and put your coat on or we will be forced to do it for you and that will be most undignified for a lady of your standing."

The interview room was crowded. Mrs. Palmer and her solicitor sat on one side of the table and Jones and Smith sat on the other. WPC Jenkins stood against one wall with DC Masters against the door. When charged, Mrs. Palmer refused to confess to murder but commented.

"Obviously you know about William and my visit to Baxter House. You know about the blackmail and now you will know that probably my William did run that young man down killing him. You also know that I drive and am familiar with the country back roads. What more do you need?"

When asked how she did it she continually repeated.

"That dreadful man took away my husband and so my life and he got what he deserved. That was justice. I don't care what happens to me I am already dead."

"How did she actually manage to kill Blount and then do what she did to him?" asked Smith later as he and Jones had a late lunch.

"We think that her husband had told her about Blount before he took his life. Then when she learned that everything she thought she had was gone, she simply decided on revenge. She made arrangements to meet Blount just as her husband had. She had a car and she knew of Baxter House and the tunnel. She arrived at the meeting place, which happened to be the local church, and using some pretence managed to get Blount to sit in her car. Possibly she made some excuse to reach into her handbag. Picked up the syringe and drove it into Blount's thigh rendering him immediately immobile. She had it well planned and was very methodical and patient. We have to assume that she went back to the tunnel later, after she had sorted out the cars. He would have bled out by then and she could set about the cutting. Quite possibly, given her state of mind, that's something we might never know."

"But why the cutting?"

"Again, unless she tells us we'll never know. Most probably she was out of her mind with grief. We know he was in the wheelbarrow just as Masters had surmised. Then I suppose she ran him down through the tunnel and used the kitchen table as her cutting board."

"Did she say why she left him like she did?"

"No, she refuses to say anything about the actual crime. It's almost as if she has forgotten what she did. Perhaps she will never remember. Perhaps that is what the judge will decide, and she will be put away at Her Majesty's Pleasure for the rest of her life."

"What about Bertha Rowington?"

"I did apologize to her, but she is still very upset at the whole business. Although very relieved that she and her daughter are now free of Blount. They left together."

Both men sat quietly for a few minutes contemplating the end result of a very troubling case. Then abruptly Smith grabbed his raincoat.

"If it's okay with you I'd like to go home now. I have to see what our young Tony has been up to today."

"Okay Jack. I'm on my way too. See you tomorrow. Oh, don't forget we have a meeting first thing with the ACC."

"How could I forget that," laughed Smith over his shoulder as he punched his way through the swing doors.

Within minutes Jones was threading his way through the narrow streets around the station heading up towards the old Clock Tower. He wanted to let Shady Lane know that the Blount case was now one for the books and to offer his thanks by means of Shady's favourite brew. Then he planned to pick up his car, pick up his date and enjoy a cosy supper at his favourite country pub.

The End

Manufactured by Amazon.ca
Bolton, ON